Winter Solstice

Seasonal Short Stories

By

Nancy MacLean

WINTER SOLSTICE
Published by Fredbagel Books
(Nancy MacLean)
njmacleanauthor.webs.com

Print version ISBN: 978-0-9921190-6-5

Electronic version ISBN: 978-0-9921190-7-2

To my friends and family, thank you for the old memories of seasons past and new memories of those yet to come.

WINTER SOLSTICE

Days shriveled and nights swelled. To save candles and lamp oil they continued to eat supper at dusk, followed by a half-hour of reading by Jo. Then they would pull across the blanket that separated the cabin into two – White and Matt on one side, and Jo and Becca on the other.

Before it had turned so cold, White had often given into Matt's constant pleas to join him on the range. And as much as he did enjoy the lad's banter at times, he craved the open space more and more and wondered how he could have lost his senses to the point he had agreed to let them stay the winter.

So, using the excuse of the increasing cold, and Matt's thin coat that now exposed bony wrists below the cuff, coupled with the lessons on numbers and reading Jo was giving the children, White was able to escape into the daylight, returning only just before nightfall.

On a particularly bleak day, after a hasty swallow of not-hot-enough day-old coffee, he grabbed a chunk of hard tack and a piece of jerky and headed outside toward the lean-to that sheltered the horses. He was glad it was

Huff's turn as the feisty mare was years younger than his gelding Poke and White needed a hard ride today. He was just pulling the cinch tight when a shadow to his left caused him to start.

"Sorry," Jo said, her soft voice nearly swallowed by the nearby forest. She shivered in her shawl and White swallowed impatience at her being cold, or at her intruding his space, probably both. She must have sensed his irritation, as she faltered in her speech. "I – I need you to take the children with you today."

"What?" He hated the ire in his voice and he tried to soften his next words. "You know Becca won't get on a horse. And I need to check on the herd." He added the last bit quickly, as it was not really the truth. Thanks to the snow-clearing Chinooks, ranchers in Alberta could often leave their herds to pasture on the plains all winter and not check on them until spring,

"You could walk," Jo went on. "Take them off somewhere not too far, build them a fire, have a lunch."

"Now why would I want to do that?" His voice had roughened again. Since fleeing across the border years before, he had prided himself on keeping his feelings inside and speaking few words. Yet this woman he hardly knew managed to pull both words and emotion from him.

She rubbed her palms on her skirts, as if they were sweating, but it was much too cold for that. Her hands returned to clasp the shawl about her. "Christmas is next week. I want to make them something. And I need to do it while the weather allows you to take them outside."

"Christmas?" It was something he did not believe in and had managed to avoid for several years.

"Yes. Please. I want to do this. Tom, I need to do this." With these last words, her eyes hardened and brightened, a nearly wild look. Maybe she too needed something to break the routine that could possibly break her before spring arrived.

White sighed. Something he was doing more of late, his patience shortening along with the days. "You want us gone all day?"

She nodded and relief washed away the hard lines of her face. "Becca's packing a lunch. I'll go fetch the children."

He watched her race to the cabin, her feet leaving no mark or sound upon the frozen ground. So, she had expected him to agree just as she had managed to talk him into letting them stay the winter.

Christ, had he no backbone against this woman?

* * *

When they returned home at dusk, a faint smell of ginger greeted them, making White's stomach growl for a sweet, something he also hadn't experienced in years. The air inside the cabin felt surprisingly cool, as if a window or door had been left open, no doubt to dissipate the cooking odors.

Matt and Becca kept quiet as they began to pull off the extra clothes they had donned for the day. It was not like Matt not to comment on the smell of food. Becca must have managed to shush her brother and she was the only one who seemed capable of that.

White opened the door to the stove to find it had been recently stoked with wood that was just catching nicely. He straightened up and found Jo unusually close to him.

"Thank-you, Tom," she whispered and gave him a rare smile, one so genuine it reached down into his soul and tickled life into a spot he thought forever dead.

He stepped back and nodded, turning away before

she could know that he was glad for her thanks, glad for the day. With his endless chatter, Matt had entertained them the whole way. Over a campfire he had panfried biscuits, just like when the children had first popped into his life. And they had eaten them with as much enjoyment and gusto as back then, when they'd been near starving.

But the warm feeling from the day had dissipated by the time he went to check on the horses. Large flakes of snow drifted downward. Large flakes, small storm, his grandmother had always said. Such rules didn't follow on the open plains, and he blamed the mountains to the west for the unpredictable weather. He could only hope it would not snow much. Just the thought of being cabin-bound erased the sliver of calm left over from the day.

His unease persisted well into the night. White knew by the pregnant silence interspersed by the odd rustle of straw, that the others were finding sleep as elusive as he. Matt seemed always to be the first to fall asleep, and sometimes, it was the lad's soft snore that helped White ease into unconsciousness. But tonight he spent longer than usual staring into the logs above him. When dawn finally stole through the lone window, the last thing he felt like doing was leaving the waning warmth of the bed and crossing the few frigid yards to stoke the stove.

But as usual, once awake, he had the urge to flee the confines of the cabin and seek the solitude that had been his companion for so many years.

As he stepped outside, he realized his grandmother had been proven right once again. Only a few inches of snow had fallen and most of that had been coaxed by the wind into crevasses and hollows so that the prairie, from a distance, looked nearly bare.

He harnessed Poke and headed out to check on the herd. The wind remained bitter, though, and he steered

Poke toward the brush to his left. After a glare from Poke that said he didn't appreciate either the saddle or White's big frame and most likely preferred little Matt who rode bareback, the gelding plodded toward the brush.

White heard a rustle and spotted a flurry of feathers. Prairie grouse. A tasty alternative to jerky. He slipped out his knife as he dismounted. He waited. Listened. Since leaving the city life as a young man, he'd soon learned that while his big hands made holding a gun awkward, they fit well around the handle of the large knife he kept sheathed to his leg. Hours and days of practice had given him a fairly accurate aim with it.

He picked up a twig and threw it into the bushes ahead of him. When he was rewarded with movement, his knife flew from his hand with purpose, as if it had a mind of its own. He was rewarded with a squawk. He pulled his shotgun free and stole into the brush. He spied his target flopping just ahead of him. He stepped carefully into the pile of snow the wind had drifted there. Maybe, just maybe there'd be a few more he could shoot. His leg sunk into a hole obscured by the snow and he was flung forward. Frozen branches scratched at his face and tugged at his clothing as he flailed for footing. His right hand snagged on a branch and the shotgun fired with a boom that made his ears ring, but didn't obscure the flutter and flap of many wings as the grouse fled in fear. Ire kindled within him. A large flock, and he had managed to kill only one, with his knife at that.

He let himself spew a few of the many curses he'd heard in his bunkhouse days – no sense being quiet now, and pushed through the brambles. A few yards away, he found the now still form of the hen his knife had found. He sliced off the head and drained the blood. Its small form would not provide much meat and he wondered if it was worth bringing home at all.

He swung about, looking for the best way out of the brush, when he spotted a blotch of red a few yards away. He bullied his way to it and found another grouse, its head nearly torn off by buckshot. He looked around. There, another one fluttered about with a broken wing. He found one more before he made his way back out to Poke.

He could not help but smile. His stumble had netted more birds then he would have gotten with his poor aim. They would make a right tasty meal. Even though there were a couple hours of daylight left, he steered Poke towards home.

His smile threatened to return once more when Jo let out a "oh my" of wonder, and Becca actually squealed in delight.

"Good shooting!" Matt said, and White thought, if you only knew.

Jo looked up at him, her brow wrinkled in worry. "How do I prepare them?"

Before White could answer, Becca took two of the birds from him. "I know. I helped my aunt with her hens. We have to dunk them in boiling water then the feathers come off easy." She looked up at White. "Would you build me a fire outside? They will stink to high heaven when we set them in the water."

So White, with Matt's help, formed a ring of stones near the woods, away from the wind, and built up a fire. While the pot boiled, White used spruce bows to form a windbreak, as the sun had set, and a cold wind threatened to steal the heat from the fire. Even Matt helped pluck while White kept the fire big and hot by adding kindling and spruce bows.

When the last bird was hoisted proud and naked by Matt, he asked. "Can we cook them now?"

White was about to bark an affirmative when Jo said,

"No, we'll save them for Christmas Day."

White swallowed a groan. This Christmas thing was getting to be a mighty pain.

Jo handed him the birds. "Here, can you hang them up somewhere, where they'll be safe until Christmas?"

Still irked by the wait, he hung them beneath a rafter in the lean-to, where they'd be frozen solid before morning.

He swore under his breath. Christmas. A lot of fuss over nothing.

By the time they'd had supper, no doubt all of them thinking of chicken rather than the beans in front of them, and finished the nightly reading, it was much later than usual by the time the candle was extinguished. The others fell asleep quickly.

But not White who worried what else this Christmas thing might bring.

* * *

Two days later a snow squall snuck into the area and dumped several inches of snow on the ground. It was slow going even for Huff to reach the herd. Damn, White thought as he studied the plains. Though the prairie wool lay beneath just beneath the snow, the cattle were too dumb to use their hoofs to break through to it. So, he and Matt spent three days bundling up hay and taking it out to the herd. Hopefully a Chinook would come soon and clear the fields.

That night at the supper table, Jo brought up the dreaded holiday again by announcing the following day would be Christmas Eve.

White continued to eat his beans as if he hadn't heard.

"So are we getting a tree?" Matt asked.

White paused, his spoon mid-air. "Tree?"

"Yeah," Matt said. "A Christmas tree."

White glared at Jo, hoping she would read the 'Now see what you've done?' in his eyes.

But instead she answered, "What a great idea."

White waved his arm. "And where do you suppose we put it?" His voice sounded too loud, too mean in the small cabin.

"We could get just a small one, and put it here, on the table," Becca suggested, her voice shaky with longing, her eyes impossibly big.

White blew out air. He tried to force gentleness into his voice but it still sounded like his throat was full of stones. "Look, not everyone believes in Christmas, or . . . Saint Nick. It's just another day."

Jo's chin tilted up ever so slightly. "Christmas is not just another day."

The air grew heavy, as White pondered a response, but none came to him.

"It's okay," Becca interjected, speaking quickly as if to ward off a battle. "Right after our uncle took us in, Matt and I learned there was no such thing as Father Christmas. We expect nothing."

"But what about – ow!" Matt rubbed his shin and frowned at his sister.

Jo stood up and began to collect the plates. "Becca, you and Matt wash up. I'm going to help Tom with the horses." She gathered her shawl about her shoulders and went through the door, leaving White no choice but to grab his coat and hurry after her. Knowing her shawl would provide little protection, he grabbed his duster and took it with him.

She reached the lean-to ahead of him, either to race through the cold or because she was angry. The latter, he thought, as she whirled about to face him. He tossed his duster to her, but she only threw it back, her dark eyes blazing.

"We can at least give them Christmas. The cattle will be fine for a day or two. Tomorrow, unless it is storming, I would like you to take the children in search of a tree. I don't care where we put it, but Becca's right, a small one will fit on the table."

"A really small one," White growled.

"That will do. I'll be baking a pie to go with the grouse for our Christmas meal and I expect your help in keeping Matt's hands off of it."

"Christmas is just a useless ritual," he barked. "I lost religion a long time ago."

"You may have, but I haven't and the children should be encouraged with it until they can decide for themselves. Besides, it gives us a bit of light in the darkest of winter. And people have been keeping Christmas, for what, nearly two thousand years? There must be something to it." Her face relaxed, though her eyes remained glistening and he felt a stab of panic that she might be about to cry. Without another word, she took his duster from him, pulled it about her shoulders, and left.

Her words remained long after she left. Poke and Huff snuffled their agreement as they chewed their hay.

As White lay in bed that night, after he could hear the three different breathing rhythms that were already so familiar to him, he tried to find an argument for her words.

But none came.

* * *

Right after breakfast, Jo set the tin of flour onto the table with deliberation. There was no mistaking the look in her eyes. White had been hoping for a storm, but with the absence of wind moaning about the eaves, and sun making the frost on the windowpane sparkle, he knew what to expect when he opened the door.

A brilliant, clear, calm day. But the air was sharp. "Brrr," he said, with exaggeration.

"Put extra layers on, children," Jo said, and tossed White a smile so quick that if he hadn't been looking right at her he might have missed the brilliance created by her excitement.

"Do we need to pack a lunch?" he asked.

"It won't take you long. Come back whenever you want, just not without a tree."

White sighed, wondering how a woman half his size could render him so docile. With Becca wrapped in Jo's shawl, and Matt wearing White's duster, they left the cabin, looking, with their heads swathed in scarves, like two adults without legs.

He shouldered the ax and led the children through snowdrifts to the nearby clump of forest where a few evergreens sprouted midst the poplar and birch.

"There!" Matt raced to a pine that reached White's shoulders.

"No," Becca said through a hole in the folds of her scarf. "It has to be small enough to set on the table." Her eyes focused and she headed to a small spruce. In spite of its two-foot stature, it had a perfect shape that tweaked White's memory of a tree in his childhood. His grandmother had always had a huge tree in the sitting room, just off the foyer, lit by a multitude of candles.

As if reading his thoughts, Matt said, "It's too small to hold even one candle."

"We won't be wasting any candles on it anyway,"

White said and immediately regretted he sounded so stern.

"We can make a paper star to put on top," Becca said. "And . . ." She scurried off the path. "Come, Matt and help me berries to put on the tree."

Matt handed White the tree and went after his sister as fast as the snow allowed. White followed when he heard an "Ow!" from Matt.

"Watch the thorns," Becca said, her voice sounding too motherly for her years.

White studied the now leafless sticks the children were plucking the few red berries that had survived the wind and snow. He didn't know what kind they were, only that they were not edible, else the birds would have finished them off. Bushes like these were common along the fringes of the few forests that neighboured the rivers and streams and sported aromatic pink flowers through the summer.

Another delectable odor greeted them when they entered the cabin and it came from a pie cooling on the top shelf. Peach, White thought, and his mouth watered. Matt went right over to the shelf and stared up at it like a starving coyote beneath a hunk of fresh-cut venison.

White picked up the lad and together they leaned in so they could both smell it. Yep, peach. Made from canned peaches, but a pie none-the-less.

"Do we have to wait until tomorrow?" Matt moaned his words.

"Yes we do," Jo said firmly. "Anticipation is part of Christmas."

Matt groaned. "I don't even know what that means."

"It means expecting and waiting for something to happen," White said and set the lad down. He knew by Jo's quick look that she hadn't expected him to know what it meant either.

As White sat down at the table, he noticed two pieces of paper folded beneath the small tree, one labeled JO and the other TOM.

Matt caught his eye. "You can't read them until tomorrow. Just like I can't have any pie 'til then."

A laugh escaped White's lips. It felt foreign to him.

"My goodness, Mr. White, did I detect some mirth?" Jo said as she spooned beans onto his plate.

"Hey," Matt said, "it's just like in the Christmas story, where the wise men brought incense and mirth."

White let himself laugh again and Jo joined him, while Becca corrected her brother. "It was frankincense and myrrh."

Matt just frowned and shrugged as he continued to shovel beans into his mouth.

"I'm not reading tonight," Jo declared. As the children began to protest, Jo went on. "Instead, I will tell you a story. The Christmas story."

White suppressed a groan and stood up. "I'd better go check on the horses," he said.

"We will wait for you," Jo offered.

"No, you go ahead." What he didn't need was a dose of religion. Besides, the sooner to bed the sooner they could get Christmas over with. Out in the lean-to he fretted over what he had seen beneath the tree. Becca must have put them there while Matt and he were ogling the pie. Some kind of 'gift' they had made for him and Jo. Jo had something to place beneath the tree as well. And what did he have? Nothing.

It took a while for everyone to fall asleep. Then White heard the soft shush of the blanket being moved aside. As a match flared, he shut his eyes against the candlelight and pretended to sleep. Tins clinked, followed by a rustle at the table. When darkness returned, he could hear the blanket being slid back into place. After what seemed like hours, Jo's breathing joined that of the children's.

White slipped out of bed and lit the lantern, keeping the flame low. He listened. Beyond the blanket, he heard two distinctive breaths. Beside the notes beneath the tree lay three small items wrapped in what looked like portions of a dishcloth. He carefully unwrapped one. Gingerbread in the rough form of a man. Or so he guessed from the two lumps with smaller thin ones attached. He sniffed. Yep. Gingerbread. Carefully, slowly, he bit down on a leg or it could have been an arm. It was hard, so he let it soften in his mouth before he finished his bite. Although it took some time to soften before he could chew, it was sweet, delicious, and it took a lot of resolve for him not to take another bite. He carefully rewrapped it and set this one a little closer to where he usually sat.

He picked up the square of paper marked Tom. It had been torn out of a book Jo had bought in town that she wrote recipes in. He opened the paper as quietly as he could. On the top were two drawings of Christmas trees. One rather well done, another looking a bit rough.

It had been a long, long time since anyone had made anything for him, and the drawings and the cookie stirred a warmth within him that felt so foreign it seemed brand new. Below the drawings were words, a few printed quite neatly, then a few more crooked, but no less poignant.

DEAR TOM

THANK YOU FOR TAKING US IN. WE PROMISE TO BE GOOD, NOT COMPLAIN, AND WORK AS HARD AS WE CAN. FOR AS LONG AS YOU LET US. THIS IS OUR GIFT TO YOU. MERRY CHRISTMAS

BECCA AND MATT

White swallowed. They had given him something more precious than anything that could be bought. A promise. And he had nothing to give in return. Or did he? He stole over to the shelf and reached behind the tins for Jo's book and the pencil inside it. He shoved both inside his shirt, slipped on his boots, grabbed his coat and hat and the lantern, and slipped into night air so frosty it took his breath away.

He hurried over to the lean-to and sat down in Poke's stall, as near to the gelding's big warm belly as he could. Poke barely gave him a glance, whereas Huff would have surely given him a swift kick for invading her space.

White turned up the lantern and withdrew the book. From the lines of prose, he could tell it contained something other than recipes and, sensing that this was something Jo did not want to share, he hastily flipped to the back where a few pages had already been torn out, He tore out another one and ripped it in half.

He thought a moment. Matt had always eyed White's knife, though he had not touched it since cutting his hand on it in the fall. So his gift to Matt would be to show him how to safely use the knife and how to throw it.

Becca refused to ride on anything that went faster than a turtle in mud, or so Matt had said. So White would help her lose her fear of horses and teach her to ride. These things he could give them.

He hesitated before he started to write, knowing putting words to paper would reveal to Jo that he was educated. His fine script would tell even more, so he elected to print in block letters. He folded the notes, labeled them, and slipped them into his pocket.

Now Jo. What in hell could he give her? He knew so little about her, other than that she came from money and had led a sheltered life. Until now, that is. So what could he possibly give to someone like that? She liked Christmas, so maybe letting them have Christmas was enough. This thought sparked another, and he picked up the lantern and strode into the far corner of the lean-to where beneath a mound of straw he kept a chest from his past. A past where Thomas White didn't exist.

In the bottom he found what he was looking for. A leather-bound bible. His grandmother had given it to him when he turned twelve. He brought it to his nose. It still smelled of her, of his life in the city. Inside was the inscription made out to Jonathan. If Jo questioned that, he would tell her the truth, that Jonathan was his first name and Thomas his middle name.

He turned the lantern low and returned to the cabin. After replacing the book and pencil, he wrapped the bible in a dishcloth and placed it and his notes beneath the tree.

He turned down the lantern and slid in next to Matt, grateful for the boy's heat. Filled with a foreign excitement, he found himself thinking about the next day. For breakfast, he would make them tea to dip the gingerbread in, and sweeten the children's tea with a bit of precious canned milk and molasses. He would build a fire in the pit outside, and cook the grouse on a spit and place potatoes and turnips into the coals along the edge. Then they would have the pie for dessert. After supper, he would ask Jo to read the original Christmas story from the bible to the children. She would like that, he was certain she would.

He lay there animated, wishing it were morning and he realized Jo had been right. Anticipation was part of Christmas. Why was he feeling it now, for maybe the first time since his childhood? As soon as he formed the question in his head, he knew the answer. He was looking forward to giving his gifts and seeing their reaction when they got them.

Maybe this was why Christmas had lasted so long, not just because most people still believed in God, but also because it gave people the same feeling he was enjoying right now. The pleasure of giving.

He focused on the warmth riding within him, and sought sleep.

Christmas was coming, after all.

And he couldn't wait.

CHRISTMAS AT SEASIDE

Everything was going wrong. Horribly wrong. On the most important day of the year.

For Diana, Christmas didn't come on Dec. 25th. It came on the second Wednesday of December when the Seaside Nursing Home held its Christmas party for the patrons.

After her divorce eight years before left her financially independent, Diana had gleefully retired and jumped into volunteer work, her most favourite being the organizer of Seaside's Christmas party. For seven years, she had pulled off the party without a single hiccup.

Well, today hiccups were popping up everywhere, the latest being the stalled traffic in front of her. She exhaled exasperation as the wipers struggled against heavy snow that defied the previous night's forecast.

The first hiccup had been a rather persistent virus that took up residence in her nasal passages more than a week ago. Most of her symptoms had subsided to where she no longer considered herself contagious, but the persistent dry cough had kept her awake enough nights in a row that last night she had decided to take two cold tablets before going to bed. Unused to taking anything stronger than a low dose of aspirin, she'd overslept. By more than three hours.

For the first time ever, she wouldn't arrive at the home in time to help decorate the dining room. She called Sandy the recreation therapist to see if she would be able to decorate without her. Sandy had responded with her perpetual cheer that it would get done in time for the dinner tonight. First hiccup resolved.

At a frantic pace that made her appreciate the extra hours of sleep, she prepared her signature cranberry sauce then picked up the phone to make her annual confirmation calls, the first being to Izzie, the caterer. As usual, efficient Izzie was at Seaside already, checking on the progress of the meal while arranging the sweets onto plates. Secondly, Diana called the bandleader who she was developing a bit of a crush on after learning he was recently divorced. He told her he was gathering his gear at that very moment. So far so good.

Then she called Fred, their Santa for the party, but there was no answer. She tried not to worry. Maybe he and his wife had gone shopping. Or he could have gone early to Seaside to sample a few of Izzie's delectable squares.

By the time she showered and dressed in her new Christmas blouse and dress pants which she hoped would make her look slim and perhaps catch the eye of a certain bandleader, it was time to leave for Seaside.

She'd stepped outside to discover a good six inches of snow blanketed her vehicle. She hurriedly brushed off the car, telling herself she still had time to reach Seaside before the meal began.

Then, for the first time since purchasing the vehicle, her engine refused to turn over for. She called CAA and her day continued its downward spiral: it would be over an hour before they could come and boost her car. She tried to phone a cab, but, in spite of trying several companies, could only get a busy signal. She had no choice but to phone CAA back and wait for them to come.

When she eventually got on the road, traffic was moving so slowly, she feared she would not arrive in time to help hand out the dinner, something she loved doing. The home provided the basic Christmas meal for the party: roast turkey, mashed potatoes, stuffing, and steamed vegetables. From the beginning, Diana had added to that with her cranberry sauce. She sighed and glanced into the back seat at the large plastic tub, its red contents staring at her as if it was all her fault.

But it wouldn't be the end of the world if she missed the dinner, she tried to convince herself. This worry blossomed into a much worse scenario when the traffic snarled to a halt before she even reached the rotary.

The car ahead of her inched ahead, but it proved to be an empty promise, a tease to both her and her idling car. There was nothing she could do, she told herself. But after so many successful parties, this pill was not easily swallowed.

In an attempt to soothe her fraught nerves, she thought back on the past seven years.

After taking over, she had contributed more to the party each year, all at her own expense, both because she could afford it and because she wanted to. The fact it would have bothered her ex-husband to know where the dollars her lawyer had managed to wrench out of his greedy hands were being spent was just a secondary benefit.

First thing she'd done was to hire Izzie to provide a full sample of home-baked goods, including sugar free and gluten-free pastries so that every one of the patrons could enjoy a taste of Christmas.

The second year, she signed up Fred, a mall Santa who made the costume and beard look real, with jolly blue eyes and a belly laugh that belonged in a children's story.

The following year, to replace the piped-in Christmas music, she booked a live band. Even those patrons who weren't mobile enough to get up and dance seemed to enjoy the music more.

Each year she purchased new decorations to compliment the old ones. Sandy had assured her that this year each and every inch of available space on the walls and tables would be decorated. Diana couldn't wait to see the room.

The car ahead of her surged forward, and she stepped on the gas, only to have to brake seconds later. If not for the anti-skid feature of her vehicle, she would have slid into the car in front of her. The large red bag on the seat beside her rolled into the dash with a soft thud.

She looked wistfully at the bag. Surely, she would get there in time for Fred to hand out the gifts. This year of all years.

She had come to know each and every patron, and each fall she made a point of meeting the new arrivals. This year, she'd used this knowledge to buy each of them a small gift instead of getting another volunteer to buy random, generic gifts. This had been more time consuming than she'd planned, but she had wanted each gift to mean something to the person receiving it. A clock with large numbers. An address book. A pair of warm socks. A nice pen. A huge calendar to write each day's events on. A package of pipe tobacco that couldn't be smoked but could still be smelled. A phone with large numbers. A battery-lit candle. Each gift was purchased with a particular patron in mind. She'd thoroughly enjoyed amassing and wrapping the gifts and couldn't wait to watch them get opened.

She frowned at the line of cars ahead of her; the string of red lights belonged on a tree, not on a street.

The car ahead moved forward. Diana eased to close the space. Dare she hope? The rotary came into view. But the traffic draped around it was stalled and too soon she was brought to a halt once more.

She sighed and pulled out her cell phone. Technically, as she wasn't moving, it shouldn't be illegal to make a call. Besides, how could anyone see inside her car with the snow so heavy?

Izzie answered so cheerfully, Diana regretted having to pass along the bad news.

"First my car wouldn't start, and now I'm stuck in traffic. Heaven knows when I'll get there. Have they finished eating yet?"

"Just about. Take your time and get here when you can. Don't worry about your cranberry sauce – I can use it at another function tomorrow."

"Have you had a peek at the room?"

"It looks fabulous! Sandy did an amazing job."

"What about the band? I told them if they showed up early they could eat with the patrons."

"They've eaten and have their gear all set up. The lead singer was asking about you, by the way."

Diana allowed her darkening mood to have its way. "He knows I'm the one with the check. Has Fred arrived yet? There was no answer at his place when I called earlier."

Izzie's voice lost some of its cheer. "Sorry, Diana, I haven't seen him. Not yet, anyway."

"Oh no!"

"But I wouldn't worry just yet." The perpetual

optimist, Izzie went on, "He's probably stuck in traffic like you are. Besides, he doesn't need to be here until the band takes their first break so there's lots of time for him to arrive. I've set aside a few sweets for him."

Diana was about to warn her friend that it was possible neither of them would make it in time, when the cars ahead began to move.

"Oh, traffic's moving. Gotta go!"

This time it kept moving, albeit slowly. There were three fender-benders along the way, though thankfully none of them seemed serious. When she finally pulled into Seaside's parking lot, she bolted inside as quickly as the heavy red bag would allow.

Music greeted her, the smooth voice of the lead singer urging her onward. She glanced at her watch and felt a waft of relief for the first time that day. She had arrived in time for the break. In time for Santa to hand out the gifts.

The moment she had her coat hung up, Sandy appeared at her side. "So glad to see you! I just got a call from Fred's wife at the hospital. They're putting a stint in and he'll be home before the weekend. Isn't that great?"

Diana stopped in her tracks and set down the sack that now felt too heavy to carry. Fred, in the hospital? No Santa? The day couldn't possibly go more wrong.

Before Diana could moisten her dry mouth enough to verbalize her anxiety Sandy picked up one side of the bag and dragged it and Diana toward the kitchen doorway.

"Good job getting another Santa on such short notice!" she bubbled over her shoulder.

"What?" Diana pulled back on her end of the bag. Then she caught sight of a large form in red taking up most of the space between the stove and the counter.

The big man turned around just as he popped a

Nanaimo bar into his mouth. He wore no glasses, but his blue eyes twinkled as merrily as any Santa's ever had. He swallowed, and his ensuing laugh boomed about the kitchen.

"Here you are!" he bellowed at Diana, his voice every bit as deep as his laugh. "And just in time!"

He grabbed the sack from Diana and slung it over his shoulder as if it weighed nothing and headed into the dining room just as the band began to play "Here Comes Santa Claus."

At that moment, Diana knew that everything was going to be all right.

She entered the dining room and affirmation of this thought flowed through her. Never had the room looked so festive. Someone turned the lights up to herald Santa's arrival, and maybe it was this that made everything sparkle: the wall decorations, the centerpieces, the patrons' Christmassy sweaters and vests. The room oozed happiness. Glee. Cheer.

But what swelled Diana's heart most was the light sparkling out of the patrons' eyes.

The big man weaved between the tables toward the back of the room with an ease belying his heft.

"Ho, ho!" he bellowed. "Any more of Izzie's squares and I'm liable to get stuck."

He knelt beside a table and pulled a present out of the bag and presented it to Flo, a diminutive lady who was very hard of hearing yet refused to wear her hearing aids.

But she must be wearing them tonight, Diana thought as Flo tipped her head back and laughed so hard at something Santa said that Diana worried the senior would fall off her chair.

Santa took lot longer than usual to go about the room, spending a few minutes with each patron and making them at least smile, if not laugh out loud. Those nearby leaned forward in their chairs, eager to have their turn.

"What a great party," said a soft voice behind Diana. As she turned around, her shoulder brushed the chest of the bandleader. He did not back away. She guessed him to be in his late fifties, like her, but his soft brown eyes twinkled with youth or mischief, perhaps both. What she had thought was a minor crush blossomed into something she had not felt in years.

"Thank you." To hide her blush, she turned back to study Santa.

"The energy in this room, it's something else," he added.

She nodded in agreement, afraid she might say something that would make him move away and take his warmth with him.

"Where on earth did you find such a great Santa?" he asked.

Relieved he was continuing the conversation, she allowed herself a glance back at him. "Our usual Santa must have asked him to fill in, I guess. I don't know who he is."

"He must be a magician or something."

Diana braved a direct look at the singer. The gentle features held no hint of teasing or joking. "What makes you say that?"

"Watch him. He just reaches into the bag and hands it to the patron, calling them by name without ever glancing at the tag on the present."

Certain the singer was exaggerating, Diana watched. Sure enough, each and every time, Santa did just that. She glanced about the room, expecting to see the patrons open the wrong gifts. But no, each handpicked gift had been accurately delivered to the right person.

Finishing at the last table, Santa sprang to his feet. If his knees were old, it was not evident. He made his way toward the door with his "Ho, ho, ho!" echoing throughout the room.

As he passed Diana, he handed her the now empty sack. "Well done, Dee!" Then, with a wink, he disappeared around the corner.

Dee? The only people to ever call her that were her parents, now long deceased. A light touch on her elbow made Diana realize the singer was still talking to her.

"Sorry, what?"

"I . . . " For the first time he looked uncomfortable. "I was wondering . . . would you want to meet for maybe a cup of coffee. . . or something?"

She blinked into the brown eyes, now worried she would wake up and find herself still stuck in traffic.

"It's okay to say no," he added quickly.

The lights dimmed just then, and he headed back to the stage, leaving Diana standing there.

Sandy startled her by slapping her shoulder. "You did it again! You made a great party even better than the year before."

Diana looked about the room. Though Santa had left, his magic remained. Everything still felt and looked surreally bright. The patrons, every one of them were all moving to the music, either on the floor with a partner, or in their chairs at the tables. Their smiles were as brilliant as any child who had gotten exactly what he wanted for Christmas.

The Santa mystery could probably be explained. Fred, or someone else, had called in a replacement who also happened to know everyone here. Someone who had excellent eyesight and quick hands. And someone who knew Dee when she'd been a child. If she tried hard enough, she would no doubt be able to learn who this

Santa was.

But she didn't need to know. She didn't want to know. Thanks to Santa, the day that had started out so wrong had ended up so right.

And it was not over yet.

She had the chance to make it even righter.

She turned, walked up to the front of the stage and stood directly in front of the lead singer. Though he kept singing, he held her gaze.

Yes, she mouthed and to make sure he understood, she nodded with deliberation.

It took a full second, long enough for self- doubt to germinate, before he grinned so broadly he had to pause in his singing.

Elated, she swung back to the room and let the magic draw her in.

Christmas had come to Seaside and everything could not be more right.

SEEING CLEAR

Lou Penderton glanced at his watch. Thirty minutes to get to a meeting ten minutes away, twenty if traffic was heavy. He interrupted his assistant's apologies with a gruff, "Forget it, I'll grab a cab." An inner voice told him it wasn't Traci's fault the limo had broken down, but he ignored it and hurried through the revolving door into a dreary December day.

Although the gaudy blue and orange vehicles typically patrolled the downtown in droves, during the next few minutes only one cab passed by, and that one occupied.

Large flakes of snow began to materialize out of the damp air. They multiplied, forcing him to brush the wet accumulation from his shoulders and hair. His peripheral vision caught a flash of orange and blue and he stepped toward the curb.

A lad raced by, narrowly missing him. Another struck his shoulder, spinning him about. Before he could utter his preformed expletive, he was blindsided by what felt like a refrigerator and did a face-plant into unforgiving

sidewalk. Holding his throbbing head, he looked up to
see the blurred forms of three youths disappearing
around the corner, obviously intent on keeping their
misled agendas.

After a round of blinking failed to clear his vision, he
grabbed his nose. His glasses were gone. He groped
about, his near-sightedness forcing him to rely more on
feel than sight to find gray frames on wet cement.

A couple of high heels walked by.

"Careful!" he barked.

The heels hesitated only a moment before continuing
on.

"Thanks for the help," Lou muttered. He groped
around with increasing panic. Then his left hand closed
on a thin strip of metal. Yes! But as he wiped off the
lenses, he noticed a golden hue to the frames. They were
not his glasses. Damn. Could anything else possibly go
wrong?

In desperation, he slid the glasses on, and to his
amazement, everything came into focus. Still on his
knees, one of which protested with a sharp ache, he
continued to scan the immediate area.

A pair of well-worn sneakers paused beside him. "Are
you okay?"

"I'm looking for my glasses," Lou growled.

"Uh . . . sir?"

Lou glared up at the unwelcome spectator. The man
looked to be in his thirties and wore a wind-breaker more
suitable for warmer temperatures.

He pointed at Lou. "Your glasses . . . they're on your
face."

"These are not mine, dammit!" He continued his
search.

"Oh, okay."

Lou snapped his gaze back to the man's face,

expecting a smirk. But to his surprise, he saw only concern. Unaccustomed to empathy in any form from anybody, let alone a stranger, Lou looked away and struggled to his feet.

"Do you want me to take you to a hospital?" the younger man asked.

Lou studied him, looking for an ulterior motive. But he could only see honesty, continued concern, and a trace of fatigue. "No, I have to find my glasses." It was amazing he could see so clearly with these new ones. Just as clearly, if not more so, than his expensive progressive lenses. But even with this excellent vision, he could not see his own frames any where.

"Well, if you're okay . . ."

Lou glanced up to see the man walking toward a cab double parked, no doubt the same one he had glimpsed just before the collision. He glanced at his watch. Perhaps he could make that meeting on time. He hobbled after the fellow. "Hey, is that your cab?"

The cabbie stopped and pointed to the 'Off Duty' sign. "I just finished my shift. I only pulled over to see if you were okay."

"Listen, it's important I get to a meeting at Yonge and Bloor."

"Sorry, I promised my son I'd be home at noon."

"I'll double your fare."

The man shook his head and climbed inside.

Lou knew the merger could fall through if he did not soon show up. He yanked open the back door of the cab, shouted "Triple!" then added, "please" in a softer tone.

The cabbie turned around. "Well, I guess it's sorta on my way home."

Lou crawled in and sank his sore body into the soft seat. His trousers were torn at the knee and his suit coat felt damp. He would prefer not to show up in such a

Nancy J MacLean

disheveled condition, but that could not be helped. He then noticed the slump to the muscular shoulders of the man in front of him, indicating the kind of fatigue that comes from long hours of work. Lou felt a twinge of something unfamiliar: gratitude. This in turn led him to do something he didn't usually do: initiate idle conversation.

"Long day?" he asked.

The driver glanced in the rear view mirror. "Just finishing a double shift so I can be off until after Christmas."

"Wouldn't tips be rather generous on Christmas Eve?"

"Probably, but it only comes once a year, and no amount of money can replace time with my family on Christmas Eve."

Lou didn't know how to respond to this. When he'd been the same age, he'd been striving to make partner, and worked sixty hours a week, regardless of the time of year, preferring to work late than face hyper-active children and over-stressed adults.

His cell phone vibrated from inside his pocket.

"Mr. Penderton?" Traci's taut voice indicated she was about to deliver more bad news. He could picture her leaning toward the phone, anxious to keep everything perfect, just as he liked. She had been his executive assistant only a few weeks and he knew she still felt insecure, though in truth she was turning out to be the best he'd ever had.

He forced some friendliness into his voice. "What is it, Traci?"

"Mr. Steven's office called. He's decided to postpone further merger talks until after the New Year. I – I tried calling you a few moments ago, but you didn't answer."

I was probably busy bouncing off the sidewalk, he

thought. Damn. In the interim, both parties would likely come up with more demands. But this also was not Traci's fault, and he tried to keep his tone light. "Well, I guess I'll see you after lunch." He put away his phone and leaned forward so the driver could hear him. "My meeting just got cancelled."

"Where do you want me to drop you off?"

For the first time in years, Lou had no immediate plans. He could purchase a new suit before he returned to work. And he could probably replace his glasses at the same time, as much as he would dread the one-hour wait in what would surely be a crowded venue. "Could I trouble you to drop me off at the Eaton Centre?"

"Sure."

As the cab pulled up outside the mall, Lou noticed the meter was off. "How much do I owe you?"

The cabbie waved him off. "Nah, that's okay. I'd already called in before I picked you up. Merry Christmas."

The fact that this hard-working fellow was allowing his kindness to overrule his obvious need for money touched Lou. He pulled out two fifties and threw the bills onto the front seat. "Thanks for the lift."

"But . . ."

Lou shut the door on the continued protests, and, trying not to limp noticeably, strode into the mall with a feeling almost foreign to him: good will. Not that he refused to tip. He always tipped, not what custom dictated but what he felt the receiver deserved.

As he stepped inside the double doors, Christmas accosted him. He had never been one to indulge in the season or its attached religion and consequently saw little need in decorations, music, or shopping. So maybe it was unfamiliarity that made everything seem so bright, so busy, so loud. He inhaled deeply and cautiously forged forward, a swimmer wading into unknown waters.

The information map told him a reputable menswear store was located on the second floor. As the escalator neared the top level, enticing odors emanated from the nearby food court: French fries with cheese and gravy. Poutine. Should he? His doctor would have a heart attack if he knew. What the hell. He had to eat, and no matter what he chose to have, anything bought here would not be on his low-carb diet. What was it the cabbie said? Christmas comes only once a year, and since he planned on working over the holiday, he'd have no mashed potatoes, turkey gravy, or pumpkin pie. Surely that counted for something.

As he waited for his order to be filled, two children raced by to claim a table. They scrambled upon opposing seats, chattering excitedly about their pending visit with Santa. Five, maybe six years old, he figured. Lou envied their enthusiastic innocence. He felt a stab of sadness that he could not recall his own children looking so. But then, he had been working hard to provide for them. Since the day he entered law school, he had vowed his family would never have to endure the poverty he had suffered as a child.

He carried his tray as he searched for an empty table, wishing he could sit near the children so he could eavesdrop further on their animated chatter.

"Lou?"

He turned around. As if conjured up by his thoughts, his ex-wife stood in front of him.

Her eyes widened in alarm. "Oh my God, what happened to you?" She grabbed his arm so tightly he nearly dropped the tray. She took it from him and placed in on a table on which sat an order of fries only slightly smaller than his. She touched her fingers lightly to his forehead. "Are you okay?"

Her gentle touch radiated an intense concern that made him want to pull her into his arms. But he had given up that right ten years before. The moment Ian left home, and without any previous warning, she had asked for a divorce. Hurt by the unexplained dismissal, he had not contested it and allowed his work to consume him even more. Except for their daughter's wedding, he had not seen Leanne since and had spoken to her only on rare occasions in terse conversations barely long enough to allow the exchange of necessary information. He touched the tender spot her fingers had found and discovered a sizeable lump.

"I'm fine. I got knocked down by a couple of racing adolescents."

"What did the doctor say?" Her cashmere sweater deepened the green in her eyes. Though thicker in the middle, her figure remained elegantly slim; her thick hair, now streaked with gray and worn in a shorter cut, shone with the luster of health.

"I didn't see one."

She tugged on his elbow. "Come on. I've got the car with me. I'll take you."

"No, I'm fine."

"But you could have a concussion and you're limping."

"Just a few bruises." He pointed to the nearby table. "Is that yours?"

Guilt flushed her cheeks, and attraction tracked through him. "French Fries are the last thing I should be eating."

He pointed to his own plate. "I won't tell if you don't."

She grinned. That same grin that had made him fall in love with her thirty-five years before.

After downing a couple of fries, she asked, "How's

Cheryl?"

He inhaled quickly. He had dated one of the new associates at his firm with the sole intention of getting her to accompany him to Jen's wedding, just to show Lea he could have any woman he wanted. Shortly after discovering Lou was not the means to an early partnership, Cheryl left both him and the firm. "I haven't seen her in years."

"Oh, I'm sorry." Lea did look sorry, and he sensed her apology was as much for bringing the name up as for the ending of the relationship.

"You seeing anyone?" he asked.

"Yes. Another teacher."

Oh, yeah. After the divorce, Lea had upgraded her degree and went back to teaching.

"I'm happy for you," he said. Surprisingly, though it hurt, he *was* glad for her. She was a wonderful mother, and a kind person who deserved to be happy.

"What about you?" she asked. "You seeing anyone?"

"No. Too busy working."

"Congratulations on making senior partner." Her eyes twinkled. "Remember when we talked about you retiring at fifty? Here we are, both past sixty and both still working."

It hit him then, a stark realization that he had little life outside work. Not wanting to show just how much this bothered him, he returned the topic of conversation back to her. "Where are you teaching?"

"At a private school in North York."

"Ah, you still live in the area?"

She laughed softly, like she used to. Then he wondered at what time during their marriage she had stopped laughing like that. "Same house, actually. It's a little big for me, but it's great when the kids visit."

So, the fellow teacher hadn't moved in yet.

She sipped on her soda, then handed it to him. "Want a sip?"

Touched that she had noticed he had neglected to buy a drink, and strangely turned on that she would share hers with him, he accepted. Immediately his taste buds recognized the bittersweet residue of a diet soda. His subsequent grimace resulted in another soft laugh that made the bad taste worthwhile and also made him wonder how he could have ever let her go. "What is this?"

"Diet Coke. I rather fancy it now. It allows me to get a soda fix without the calories. Now tell me Lou, what on earth brings you to a mall on Christmas Eve?"

He knew she was referring to the fact that in lieu of gifts, he sent Ian and Jen each a cheque the first of December. Jen, being a lawyer herself and married to a dentist, probably didn't need the money, yet cashed hers each year and sent him a thank-you card. Ian, who probably lived at a near-poverty level with income from band gigs, had not cashed the cheques in all the years Lou had been sending them. He pointed to the hole in the knee of his right pant-leg. "Figured I'd better get a new suit."

"Let me guess. You plan on working late, then heading over to your sister's just in time to say good-bye to her departing guests."

She knew him well. As an only child, he had abhorred crowds and the infernal noise and sometimes arguments that accompanied them. Lea, however, had always seemed to jump at the chance to cook and entertain for others, relatives and friends, or friends of relatives and friends. Everyone welcome. Always room for an extra plate at the table.

"I'm surprised you're here," he said. "Don't you usually spend the whole day preparing a feast for that unruly clan of yours?"

"I haven't done that for some time. Everyone's busy with their own extended families. Lately on Christmas Eve it's just been the kids and their significant others. We gather in the kitchen around woks and cook up a few Chinese dishes. I got up early today, and after I got everything prepared and in the fridge, I decided to get a dose of ol' fashioned Christmas Eve chaos. I used to bring the kids to this mall when they were young because they had the best Santa Claus here, remember?"

He remembered. He also remembered how cranky he'd been, picking them up after work before threading his way through stop-and-go traffic to their home in the suburbs.

A familiar blue windbreaker passed by. The cab driver, with a younger version of himself in tow, carried a tray laden with pizza slices and sodas. As he spun about looking for a table, he noticed Lou.

Lou half-rose from his chair. "Here, you can use this table." He turned back to Lea. "We're finished, aren't we?"

Lea nodded and pulled her coat from the back of her chair.

"Thanks," the younger man said, setting his tray down. "I didn't know if I'd see you here or not." He held his hand out. "I'm Terry, and this is my son, Jason. Jason, this is the nice man I told you about."

Lou shook hands with the boy who looked to be six or seven years tall. "Hello, Jason. You can call me Lou. This is my wife, Lea . . . er, I mean my ex-wife." Dammit, he could feel himself blushing.

Terry's eyes darted between Lou and Leanne. "I hope we're not intruding."

"Not at all," Lou said. "I'd better get going anyway."

Terry frowned. "You know, I worried about you after

I dropped you off. My wife's a nurse, and she said a head injury might not show symptoms until later. You're not feeling dizzy or anything are you?"

Terry's concern and Lea's worried look caused another flush of warmth. Since his divorce, Lou had never felt less alone, and it was a wonderful feeling. "No, I'm fine."

"No blurred vision?"

"No. In fact, I've never seen clearer." Really, he thought, as he touched the frames resting on his nose. Maybe he should keep them. He turned to Lea. "Want to help me pick out a suit?"

She blinked at him, and he feared he had overstepped his bounds, that she would refuse, walk away, and that he wouldn't see her for another several years. But the enthusiasm in her "sure" matched what he saw in her eyes.

She smiled at Terry and his son. "Nice to meet you both."

Lou tried not to limp but he did not object when Lea slid her arm under his.

They had only just left the food court when Terry ran up to them. "Look," he spoke in a near whisper as he glanced back at his son, "I- I want to thank you for that tip. It means Jason and I can buy his mom something special this year."

"Don't mention it. I appreciated the lift."

"Well, Merry Christmas." He turned and rejoined his son.

Lou turned to find Lea staring up at him. "What?"

"I don't know, you seem different."

No, thought Lou, I *see* different. I see better. Since putting on these new glasses, he saw things, felt things he wouldn't have earlier. Terry's fatigue, and the love he felt for his family; the innocent anticipation of the children, and Lea, her caring heart and kind soul. A lump formed in his throat at the realization of what he had missed out on and what he had lost. No, what he had given away.

"How much time do you have before you go back to work?" Lea asked.

"How much time do *you* have?" he responded

She answered, "All afternoon."

"Just a second." He pulled out his cell phone and called his office. Traci answered before the end of the first ring.

"Hi, Traci. What's on my agenda for this afternoon?" As he spoke, Lea turned away and he could see a change in her posture, particularly a tautness between her shoulder blades. The familiarity of it made him quickly add, "Let me rephrase that. Clear my agenda, and take the rest of the day off."

Lea turned around, her eyes widening, and the corners of her mouth twitching as if trying to rein in a smile.

"Yes, I'm sure," he responded to Traci's surprised query. "Merry Christmas." Before he put his phone back in his pocket, he turned it off. Lea's broadening smile made a thrill go through him.

As they proceeded down the mall, she slid her arm into his once more and he squeezed it against his side. He set a leisurely, yet limping pace, wanting the afternoon to last forever. "You know, I used to dread being in a mall at this time of year."

"I know. You missed out on all this Christmas spirit."

"Don't you mean Christmas consumerism?"

She stopped and gave him a stern look, one he was sure she used on her students. "No, I don't. It's not the buying or the getting that lends this excited air to everything. It's the giving. Times have changed and the standard of living has changed, but the giving, and the joy it brings, hasn't, be it a toy to a child, or a full plate to someone hungry. They say Christmas is for children, but it is really for those who want to give, no matter what the age." Her smile rendered her words even more persuasive.

As they continued their stroll, he wondered if he could learn to give, really give.

Lea stopped again, her eyes widening like a child spotting a cookie jar. "Oh, look. Can we go in there?"

They stood in front of a store whose window display consisted of huge building blocks spelling 'BABY'. Lou gaped. Just a few weeks before, Jen had mentioned that she and Tom were considering having children. As she was just two years into her practice, Lou had suggested she try to land a partnership first. Okay, so she hadn't taken his advice, but he was disappointed she hadn't confided in him.

Lea peered up at him, her eyes welling with worry. "Oh, no. You don't know? I thought maybe Jen might have told you."

She looked so genuinely upset, he pulled her close for a side hug, though he wanted to do much more than that. "Hey, we're going to be grandparents! Want to collaborate on some serious spoiling?"

The wariness that came into her eyes hurt. What else could he expect, he thought, from a suggestion that they actually keep in touch, maybe even see each other? Since the night she first asked for a divorce, he had rarely spoken to her, letting the lawyers settle everything. She had been reasonable, wanting only the house, a surprisingly small monthly stipend, and his prized '77 Corvette Stingray. He figured the latter was an attempt on her part to initiate a battle that he refused to partake in.

"Really?"

Her question jerked him out of the painful past. In

her eyes, he saw that anticipation had replaced her earlier hesitation. He smiled down at her, hoping she could see his sincerity. "Really. A grandchild. Imagine."

Her grin took up most of her face. "I can hardly wait!"

Was it his imagination or had her grip on his arm tightened? He allowed his awkward stride to take him closer to her. Soon her shoulder grazed his arm with each step. He could smell her perfume, and decided he would buy her some for Christmas. He hadn't bought her a Christmas present in seven years. A tingle went through him. The joy of giving, he figured.

The sound of a piano playing Silent Night grew increasingly louder as they approached a music store. In the window, a player-piano emitted the soothing tune, its keys tickled by an invisible hand.

"Does Ian still play the guitar?" he asked, then thought, stupid question. Of course he did, if he was making a living of any kind.

"He's teaching now. Guitar and piano."

"He's not in a band anymore?"

"Oh yes. The same group, except they have a new drummer. They play at weddings and on other special occasions. But they don't tour anymore. I think the others are married and have children."

Doesn't sound like he's making much money, Lou wanted to add. But instead, he confessed, "Ian's never cashed any of my Christmas cheques."

Another soft laugh. "That sounds like Ian. He's quite stubborn, and we both know that didn't come from my side of the family. He's doing okay, though. He and his girlfriend, Abby, have been living together for almost two years, and he seems really happy."

"Good. I'm glad." And he was, in spite of all the arguments over how Ian had wasted his mathematical brain on music. At one time, a recent time, Lou conceded, he had equated money with happiness. He looked down at Lea and a thought saddened him. She was happy without him. No doubt she had stuck with his late nights, inattention, and grumpiness for the sake of the kids, and got out of the marriage as soon as she could. Good for her.

"Oh, look at the snow come down!" Lea stepped over to the floor-to-ceiling window, pulling Lou with her. Large flakes danced earthward as if in rhythm with the mall's music. Already the cars below wore white cloaks.

Lea grimaced. "Goodness, maybe I'd better head home before the roads get bad."

Disappointment sat heavy upon Lou's chest. He forced a smile. "Yes, you'd better."

She studied him a moment. "Can I give you a lift?"

"No, I'd better get that suit and head back to the office."

"Okay . . . well, Merry Christmas, Lou." Her features sported a smile, but the light in her eyes had gone out. She turned and briskly walked away.

His eyes followed her. Just before she disappeared into the crowd, he noticed the same tension in her posture that he'd seen earlier. He then realized that she had really wanted to give him a lift. He limped after her through the crowd. Being tall, he could still see her small head, the streaked hair bouncing slightly with her determined step. It turned toward the escalator. Once she reached the bottom, he could lose her.

He leaned over the railing and shouted, "Lea!" He had always been proud of his deep voice. It held authority, confidence. At the moment what he liked most about it was that it was loud.

Several faces looked up at him. To his relief, one of them was Lea's.

"Wait for me!" Her nod sent his heart skipping. During the slow descent of the shuddering escalator, it was all he could do not to bully his way through the pack. At the bottom, he spun about, looking for her. Then someone tapped his arm. She stood there, waiting. He felt tongue-tied, like at university when he wanted to ask her to dance. As then, it was the hope in her eyes that gave him the courage to finally speak.

"Could—uh—is that offer of a ride still open?"

Her smile softened into a grin. "It is. Follow me." She took his arm and led him to the elevator to the underground parking.

As soon as the doors slid open, he spotted the Corvette just a few feet away. His Corvette. "You didn't sell it?"

He could see her trying not to smile as she unlocked the passenger door. "No, I like driving it too much. I would have caught the bus though, if I'd known it was going to snow." She held the keys out to him. "Want to drive?"

Not caring if he sounded like a kid, he asked, "Can I?"

"I know you can, and yes, you may."

He grinned. "Still the school teacher, I see."

She laughed as he struggled to wedge himself down into the seat and slide it back. "I see it's been awhile since anyone but you drove this."

"Ten years," she said. "No one else. Not even Ian."

He could see the possessive determination in her eyes. Something that had not been there while the children were growing up. Good for her.

Silence ensued while they waited at the next traffic light. He struggled for something to say.

She sighed, as if coming to a resolution. "Do you know why I asked for this car?"

He wanted to look at her, but the light had turned and the congested traffic, slick streets, and stick shift took all his concentration. "Not really."

Another sigh, this one more uncertain. "I wanted to keep something that I knew you cared about."

Another lump formed in his throat, this one more resistant to swallowing. "I tend to do the opposite," he managed to squeeze out.

"Tend to do what?"

"Give away what I care about."

As they entered a ramp, he cautiously sped up. Thrilled with the throb of potency he heard in the engine's hum, he said, "She's as smooth as ever. You've taken good car of her."

"I have," Lea answered.

Something teasing in her voice made him risk a look at her. Her eyes twinkled with anticipation.

"What?" he asked.

"Where are you going?"

Without conscious thought, he had turned onto the Don Valley Parkway. Toward his former home. To where Lea still lived.

"I have no idea!" he blurted, feeling his cheeks burn. "On auto pilot, I guess. That bump on my head must have rattled my brains."

"Would you like to stay for dinner?"

Yes. Badly. But dare he?

"What about your teacher friend." He didn't want to use the word boyfriend.

"Oh, he has his own family to visit." She paused and then said, "It's nothing serious. We've only dated a few times. Please come, Jen will be thrilled."

"Yeah, but Ian won't. He might walk out."

"And he might want you to meet Abby."

Lou glanced at her, then back to the road. "You sure?

I don't want to spoil your evening."

"I've never been more sure."

Another glance ensured her sincerity. Lou wished he could have read her this easily during the thirty-one years they had been married. Maybe she wouldn't have left him.

As he turned into the driveway, the back wheels skidded slightly. Jen and Tom's SUV sat to the left of the detached garage.

"Oh, good," Lea said. "Looks as if everyone's here."

Lou's gut clenched. "Ian, too?"

Lea twisted in her seat to look at him. "Yes. Ian's car didn't start today and he called to say they'd be coming with Jen and Tom." She reached over and squeezed his arm. "Stop worrying. It'll be so wonderful for us all to be together."

She did want him there, he could see that. And the pleading in her eyes gave him hope that perhaps he'd be able to mend things with both his children. Especially with these glasses.

The walk had been shoveled, but Lou felt the ice on the surface as he stepped out of the car. As she had in the mall, Lea slipped her arm into his. Just as they mounted the first step up to the porch, she slipped. His reaching for her sent his own feet skating out of control. Together they fell into a snow bank.

Midst a flurry of giggles, she asked, "Are you all right?"

He was, as the accumulated snow had cushioned his landing, but his vision was blurry. "Damn, I've lost my glasses."

"Don't move!" she instructed. She reached over his shoulders and felt around, leaning close. Too close. He pulled her down on top of him.

She let out a squeal that sounded like it came from a teenager. "Are you crazy? You're probably lying on your glasses." Her eyes gleamed with flirtation.

He answered by kissing her. She did not pull away. A door squeaked and they both looked up. Although the porch light had come on, the door remained shut.

"Oh, found them!" Lea reached over his left shoulder then handed him his glasses. They helped each other up. As he shook the snow from the frames, he noticed their dull gray tint. They were his old glasses. "Oh no!"

"What?"

He held them up. "These are my old glasses."

"So?"

He hesitated. How could he explain to her what he couldn't understand himself? It just didn't make sense. Had he mistaken the gold tint and been wearing his own glasses all this time? No. He had seen things differently. He had felt differently. Lea stood in front of him, waiting patiently.

"It's just that with these glasses . . . well, with the other ones, I . . . I thought I could see things better. And what I saw in others I wanted to see in myself. Those glasses made me a better person."

Worry creased Lea's forehead. "Maybe I should take you to the hospital after all."

He tried again. "Look, Lea. Making partner and the prestige and money that came with it had always been my priority. Those other glasses made me realize that by forcing my ideals on you and the kids, especially Ian, I ended up pushing you all away." He sighed and looked at the frames in his hand. "And now they're gone."

She took the glasses from his hands and slid them gently onto his nose. "There. Who do you see?"

"You."

"Me. The same woman you swept off her feet so many years ago." Her eyes grew wet and she added, "And again just now."

"But . . ." he glanced at the house, "I'm scared I might not see what I need to with the kids."

She leaned close and looked up at him. "Never mind selective hearing, they should call it selective *sensing*: hearing, feeling, and *seeing*. Lou, you can see what you want to see, no matter what glasses you have on." She took his hand. "Come on. Come inside to your family."

He let her lead him up the steps, this time both of them holding onto a handrail. In all his years of corporate litigation, he could not remember being so frightened.

When they stepped inside, Jen and Ian were setting the table. Jen dropped the chopsticks she was holding, shouted, "Daddy!" and ran to him with a glowing expression that told him she was indeed thrilled he had come. Just before she reached him, she put on the breaks, and stared, first at his pants, then his face.

"Oh my god! What happened? Are you okay?"

"I'm fine. Just a minor collision with the sidewalk." As Jen hugged him, he risked a glance at Ian who continued to arrange the plates on the table although they didn't look as if they needed further arranging.

Jen's husband, Tom, came out of the kitchen holding a bottle of white wine and a corkscrew. He gathered them both in his left hand, and held out his right. "Mr. Penderton."

"Please, isn't it about time you called me Lou?"

"Okay, Lou." Though there had never been any harsh words between them, the young man looked wary.

Lou let his gaze drift to Ian. The last time he had seen him had been at Jen's wedding four years earlier. Then his hair had reached his shoulders, and he wore a goatee. Now his hair was cut in a style shorter than Lou's, and he was clean-shaven. Lou took a stab at humor and said, "Who are you and what have you done with my son?"

A woman laughed. Lou turned and saw a heavily pregnant woman standing in the kitchen doorway. "Hello," she said. "I'm Abby."

"Oh my God!" Lou exclaimed. "*You're* having our baby?"

Ian frowned and strode over to possessively put his arm around her. "No, Dad. Abby's having *my* baby."

Lou looked Lea. "I – I thought you meant Jen."

Lea gave him an apologetic smile. "I guessed that. But I didn't think you should hear news like this second hand."

Fair enough, Lou thought. Ignoring Ian's glare, he held out his hand to Abby. "I'm Lou."

Abby pushed past his hand and flung her arms around his neck. "I'm so glad you came, Lou." Her hug outlined the basketball she was carrying.

"When's it due?" Soon, Lou guessed.

"Near the middle of January. Our baby will be delivered at home with a mid-wife." Ian's voice rang with challenge.

Lou felt the air sharpen with tension.He turned to Jen, the one member of his family with whom he'd never quarreled. "So you're not pregnant."

"No, Daddy. Tom and I haven't decided yet."

"No," Tom said, "*you* haven't decided yet." His tone indicated Jen was the one holding back.

Insecurity racked through Lou. Nothing had changed. Ian still resented his input, Jen thought too much of it.

Lea came to Lou's rescue. She squeezed his hand, and the warmth hinted at what could be. She turned to Jen. "You'll know when the time is right. You'll both know," she added, tweaking Tom's cheek.

"That's right," Lou said. "That's a decision for the two of you and no one else."

Jen looked at him quizzically while Tom's features

relaxed, and Lou felt that maybe, just maybe things would be okay.

Then Ian surprised him by saying, "Dad, I'd like a word with you." His dark eyes, so like the ones Lou saw in the mirror each morning, were cold.

"I have the woks set up in the kitchen," Lea said. "The rest of us can start cooking." She herded the others ahead of her, pausing at the door to give Lou a warm smile of encouragement.

Lou took in a deep breath and turned to his son, worried about what could make Ian so angry he would talk to him.

Ian stepped close. He had grown more than a few inches since Lou had last seen him, and was able to look Lou directly in the eye. His dark brows knit as he spat out his words. "What do you think you're doing, kissing and hugging Mom like that?"

Lou inhaled sharply. "I never stopped loving your mother." Nor you, he wanted to add.

"Well, you have a funny way of showing it! Goddammit, I will not let you hurt her again."

How dare he tell him what to do? Lou's anger quickly matched Ian's. "She divorced me, remember? And I don't think it's any of your goddamn business!"

Ian nodded and stepped back. "You know? You're right. It's none of my business what you do. It never has been and it never will be. Just remember to stay out of mine." He stomped toward the kitchen.

Regret tumbled over and around Lou's hurt. Their first conversation in seven years was about to end just like their last. "Ian, wait."

But Ian didn't and disappeared into the kitchen. Black grief stole through Lou. He had been given another chance with his son, and he had let selfish hurt and anger ruin it. He could feel tears coming, and, afraid someone would see, he stepped out onto the porch, and buried his face in his hands.

He wiped his face with his handkerchief then looked at his glasses. The porch light was just bright enough for him to confirm they were his titanium ones. Had he been mistaken about the golden hue all along? He slid them back on and sucked the crisp air into his lungs. The clouds had moved off, allowing the stars to twinkle in the indigo sky. The blanket of snow smoothed every edge, every protrusion; even the silence seemed softer. He told himself he should find all this soothing, but tears continued to leak out of his eyes.

He looked at the Corvette and his hand instinctively went to his pocket. Yes, he still had the keys. Better to leave now, and give the rest of them a chance to enjoy their Christmas Eve.

He opened the car door and was about to slip inside when he saw Ian standing by the garage, his slim form thickened by a down-filled jacket.

"What, you're stealing her car, now?"

Lou blinked rapidly, hoping to disperse his tears, but the action only sent them rolling down his cheeks.

"No!" He forced gruffness into his voice. "I'm only borrowing it."

Ian stepped closer. "Borrowing it?" Resentment and mistrust deepened his voice. "You can only 'borrow' something, when you've asked the owner for permission — whoa — didn't we have this same conversation about fifteen years ago, only I was the one borrowing . . ." he leaned closer. "Are you crying?"

"NO!" Lou answered, louder than he wanted to. "What were you doing hiding there, anyway?"

"I wasn't hiding. Abby told me to go out and cool off. That's one thing I guess I got from you -- hey, you are crying."

"No, I'm not." Lou turned away and hastily wiped his face with the back of his hand. When he risked a look back at Ian, he saw puzzlement, and . . .was that concern? This only set off more tears.

"I – I've never seen you cry before," Ian said softly.

Lou gave up trying to hide them and faced his son. "Yes, you have."

Ian looked wary. "When?"

"When your mother handed you to me. You were all but four minutes old." A bubble rose in his throat and he could not keep a sob from escaping. "I was so happy."

Ian blinked a few times, then said, "Guess you couldn't have known then how I would turn out."

"No." Lou tried to find the right words, then, worried Ian would misunderstand his silence, he blurted out, "Thank God you didn't turn out like me."

Ian frowned, and shook his head as if he didn't believe what he was hearing.

The tears were gone now, and Lou found the courage to plead, "I hope you let me be a part of your child's life where I failed to be a part of yours."

Ian studied him, and Lou feared he would tell him to stay away. But instead, he said, "Okay, who are you and what have you done with my father?"

Lou laughed, filled with glorious relief. "I guess I deserved that one."

Ian laughed too, and it sounded like an echo of Lou's.

Lou said, "You know, I like Abby."

Ian grinned. "She's great, isn't she? We're going to get married right after the baby is born."

"That's terrific."

A million questions wrestled on Lou's tongue, wanting to ask about Abby's family, her background. The old Lou would have turned the conversation into an interrogation. But the new Lou tried to concentrate on the happiness he was seeing in his son. The silence grew awkward to the point Lou was thinking of talking about the weather when Ian spoke.

"Oh, and don't get overdrawn. I cashed your cheque this year. We used it to fix up the baby's room."

"You did? That's great."

Ian shut the Corvette's door. "I'm hungry. Let's go eat." On the way back to the house, he held out his hand. "And give me Mom's keys."

"I wasn't stealing it," Lou said as they mounted the steps, trying to mimic Ian from ten years earlier.

"Sure you weren't," Ian answered, doing a fair impersonation of his father.

As if she had been waiting there, Lea opened the door the moment they reached it. Her smile could not have been more brilliant. She helped Lou out of his suit coat while the others gathered at the table. Before she could step away, he cupped her elbow and drew her close. "Come here, Beautiful."

"Beautiful?" She wrinkled her nose. "I've put on weight and I'm letting my hair go gray. Maybe you do need new glasses."

"No, I don't," Lou said. "I've never seen clearer.

FOR JUST A LITTLE WHILE

Not for the first time, Wally awoke with the startling revelation that he was not in his own bed. Too soon his memory returned, confirming the reality that he wasn't even in his own home. It had been five weeks and still, he wondered how the heck he had let them talk him into selling his home and moving here.

"It's not a nursing home," his daughter Amanda had insisted. "It's called residential care."

Well, they could call it what they want, it was still an institution as far as he was concerned. Sure, he had his own room with his own bathroom and he had been allowed to bring his prized recliner and his television, but outside his door was a world in which he did not want to belong.

And dang it, they were already decorating for Christmas. Bah! They wouldn't be putting any of that tacky stuff up in his room if he had anything to say about it. He doubted his kids and grandkids would even come here. Last Christmas they all came to his house like they had been doing for several years, as he didn't like to venture outside in the cold, with the ice and snow that rendered the sidewalks a slippery slope to probable surgery. Yep, they had all come, even the squalling great grand baby. But they had only stayed just for a little while - just long enough to perform that silliest of traditions, exchanging gifts. Bah!

A knock came on the door and he swallowed the irritation tightening his throat. "Come in."

A nurse poked her head inside the door and grinned at him. "Lunch will be served in a few minutes, want me to walk you down?"

"No, I'll be down in a minute."

When Wally had first moved here, he often skipped meals. They didn't enforce strict dining times, but he soon learned that he got the best choice if he chose to eat when the other fifteen clients did. But it meant he had to share a table with three others. He kept quiet and his answers to their meddling questions short, and soon they pretty well left him alone.

He waited as late as he dared, then struck out for the dining room. To his surprise, the chair next to his sat empty. Where was Frank?

Wally sat down and fidgeted with his fork while he cursed himself for walking too fast and arriving too early. No doubt the other two, George and Thelma would want to gab with him arrived. But they remained quiet, though he could feel them exchanging glances. A conspiracy perhaps to make him talk. Well, his curiosity wasn't so great that he would feel like talking. Once he crossed that line, they would forever expect him to be a chatterbox.

Soon their food arrived, spaghetti, as it was Wednesday. It wasn't half bad, but he wished they would spice it up a little, even if the spice would make his reflux act up. He chewed slowly, waiting for the others to talk. But they remained quiet, even after desert and tea were served.

Wally slurped the final dregs of his tea, allowed himself a small burp, then reached for his cane and headed back to his room. He hadn't reached the hallway when he heard them whispering. When he glanced back they were not looking at him, but at Frank's empty chair

That night, when the nurse brought Wally his pressure pill, Wally allowed himself to cross a line and asked where Frank had gone.

"Oh, he moved into the building next door."

Wally knew what that meant. Nursing home. The next step in the perpetual decline of independence. Just one step away from the coffin, as far as Wally was concerned.

"You can go visit him, if you like," the nurse said in her cheery voice.

Wally grunted, threw the pill to the back of his throat and chased it with a swallow of water.

"He was going to have his phone hooked up – do you want to call him?"

Wally just grunted again, and turned the television on.

When the nurse stood there waiting, he turned up the volume. Once she shut the door behind her, Wally turned the volume down again. Yep, this was his fate. Suffer out his days here until he can't make it down for dinner, then it'd be his turn to go the building next door. Just shoot me now, he thinks.

The next morning, he decided to go to the exercise class that was offered each morning. Just to keep the building next door at bay, at least for a little while.

He would miss Frank, as the women far outnumbered the men and now the only other men left besides him were George and Tony. While Tony was just plain nuts and often rambled on to anyone passing by about his bowels, George was a braggart. When bands came in to play music for the residents, George would sing along, often drowning the real singers out.

Damn, Wally swore to himself when he realized neither of the other guys had shown up for the exercise class, just five women he didn't know the names of. A few greeted him, and after responding with his usual grunt, he returned to his room with the intention of a nap before lunch.

He had just nodded off when that damn young thing that looked like she just left high school stuck her head in the door and asked if he'd need help with his shower that afternoon. Shoot me now, he thought and grunted a no.

At lunch he discovered they had already filled Frank's spot with a woman. Lordy, he thought. She'll probably try to talk to him and it'll take at least three days of rudeness for her to learn to leave him alone.

Sure enough, he had just sat down when she stretched a hand across the table. "Hi, Wally, I'm Gladys."

"I just washed my hands," he growled.

The hand withdrew, and he heard a whispered, "I told you so," from Thelma.

"Well, at least, he didn't grunt," Gladys said cheerfully.

Thelma and George gasped in unison.

Wally lifted his head and bestowed upon Gladys his best attempt at an ominous glare. As she bracingly met his gaze, intelligence and a bit of sauciness shone out of her bright eyes.

"What?" he growled, intent on erasing this woman's obvious happiness to be here.

She laughed and the wrinkles around her eyes doubled, but in a way that made her look younger, not older.

She reached over and actually patted his arm. Before he could form words nasty enough to make her withdraw her hand, she said, "Thelma here says you never talk, that you just grunt. Well, you just proved you can speak clearly enough."

Thelma put her hand to her mouth. George just sat there, his mouth open, a first for George.

"Oops, now I suppose I should wash my hand." Gladys waved the hand she had touched him with.

Wally was saved from trying to find the appropriate response when plates of chicken salad were set down in front of them.

Gladys grinned mischievously. "Oh, I think I'll chance it." With the aforementioned hand, she took one of the rolls and buttered it. "Ooh, fresh rolls. I heard the food here is good."

With Thelma's answer that the food here was indeed very good, Wally worried how long it would take before he would once more be able to eat in silence. He decided to push his rudeness.

"Now perhaps you will allow me to finish my meal in peace and quiet?"

"Oooh!" Gladys cooed. "That's a mighty big sentence for a grunter."

"Now look," he began but Gladys cut him off.

"Oh, another sentence! My, this is our lucky day!"

George started to laugh, then nearly choked, and coughed so hard, Wally covered his plate with his napkin. When the two women started to titter, Wally pushed to his feet.

Gladys grabbed his arm. "I'm sorry, Wally. I love to tease. Please sit down and finish your lunch. I'll try to behave."

Her hand on his arm exuded a gentle warmth. He looked up into sincere blue eyes. Eyes that he realized were the same shade of blue as his Sadie.

"Yes," Thelma added. "We'll be good, Wally. Please stay and eat."

"Naw, let the grump go," growled George.

Between George's suggestion and the salad Wally

knew he liked, or at least he had last week, he stayed put. Besides, he rationalized, the desert today was lemon pie, his favorite.

He had only taken two bites, when Gladys spoke again. "Oh, this is good. Do you know what we're having for supper?"

"I thought you said you were going to be quiet?" Wally growled, but he couldn't quite put the sternness he wanted into his words.

"No, I said I was going to behave, not be quiet." She turned to Thelma. "Do you know what's for desert?"

"No, I forget," Thelma said.

"Jello," George boomed.

"They don't serve Jello here!" Wally didn't want to defend the place but he did want to take any opportunity to prove George wasn't as smart as he thought he was. "Lemon pie usually, when they serve this salad.

Thelma leaned toward Gladys, "I think Wally is right."

But he was proven wrong as well when they were served slices of coconut cream pie.

Wally stared at his dessert, waiting for George to gloat. But Gladys spoke first. "Oh, even better! My favourite pie in all the world." She raised her hand for service. "Could I have more tea please?" She beamed at Wally. "Don't you just love a hot cup of tea with pie?"

"I do," Wally answered, startled by the softness he heard in his voice. It was his Sadie voice. Tea and pie had often been their afternoon snack.

The responding smile Gladys gave him made what was left of his grumpiness fade. Sadie had been able to do that, to get him to be less 'snarky' as she called it. All she had to do was smile, a smile that said, I accept you, and I like you, even if you are a grumpy old fart. And it made him not want to be a grumpy old fart.

That night, when he knew the card games were gong

on, he stole down the hall and peeked around the corner. He just wanted to watch Gladys a minute, then return to his room to watch wrestling.

But that damn Thelma saw him and when she poked Gladys, he ducked back behind the wall. He was almost to his room when he felt a light touch on his arm. Gladys stood there, in his space, smiling that damn smile.

"Do you play Auction Forty-five?"

The question and her eyes threw him off. "I haven't played in years."

"Well, we need a fourth. Please come play with us."

He wanted to say no, but instead found himself saying, "I'll probably be lousy at it."

"Me too! I bet you'll look good beside me!"

Yes, I would, he thought, and allowed her to lead him to a table at which Thelma and another lady who introduced herself as Kate in a terse tone that told Wally he should have known her name by now.

He regretted coming and was about to mutter an excuse and head back toward his room, but Gladys gently grabbed his elbow and said, "I claim Wally as my partner!"

He looked at her and she added, "It's much more fun to play in pairs." She leaned close and he got a waft of mint. "We'll be ruthless," she whispered.

Oh damn, he knew he was in trouble as he sat down. For the second time in his life he had come across a woman who could bend him to her will. He'd lived 53 years with the first one. He had figured that living alone for five years had cured him of bending to anyone's will ever again. Apparently not.

They lost. In spite of George crowing victory two tables over, Wally found himself smiling, and he even laughed once. Each of them made mistakes, and the partners were often the first ones to point them out, but when Gladys pointed his out, she made it seem it was her fault, not his, and she poked such fun at herself that she had the whole table laughing.

After that, Wally didn't miss a card game, or a Wii bowling game. With Gladys's presence, the others didn't annoy him nearly as much.

Often before the meals they would do a little walk through the hallways, pausing at times to look through the windows at Winter's arrival. If a storm was coming, they would sneak each other a note at supper, and meet in the lounge after everyone had gone to bed. They would turn the couch around to face the window and sit side by side as they watched the storm.

The second such night, after they had talked about Sadie's passing, and her husband's recent one, Wally dared hold her hand. She let him.

Three days before Christmas a small band came to the residence and played Christmas music. When they struck up the song, "The first Noel," Gladys leaned against him and asked, "Would you dance with me, Wally?"

"I – I can't." He waved his cane.

"Use me as your cane," she said.

He could not say no. With a surprisingly strong hand, she led him to the back. There, with his hand on her waist, and his other grasping hers, he let her lead.

They were the only ones dancing and for once, George kept his baritone to himself. The twinkling lights, the music, all of it seemed surreal.

The music stopped and a too-thin Santa in a red jacket and stringy beard came in to give out candy.

Gladys's eyes were bright. "I hope you don't mind, I've bought you a little something for Christmas."

Relieved, Wally smiled. He'd gotten his daughter to pick up a warm sweater for him to give to Gladys, as she seemed to get cold easily. He had fretted for two nights as

to how he could get up the nerve to give it to her. He was
also grateful his thoughtful daughter had wrapped it for
him.

"I've got you something too," he said.

Gladys giggled, "How lovely! Let's exchange gifts
Christmas Eve. My family's going to pick me up
Christmas morning and take me out for the day."

"Mine's coming here Christmas day, for just a little
while."

"So how about we exchange gifts Christmas Eve
then?" Gladys's eyes reminded Wally of his children's
when they were young and had their first glimpse of the
fully decorated tree.

He nodded. "Here, after everyone's gone to bed."

"Hmmm," Gladys said. "I wonder if there's a
mistletoe to be had around here."

At this Wally laughed aloud and those residents that
could turned in their seats to see what they were up to.

The next two days could not pass fast enough for
Wally. He bribed Al the orderly to steal a small tuff of
mistletoe off the decorations at the front.

But when Wally went to supper on Christmas Eve, he
was shocked to see Gladys's chair empty. She always
arrived before he did.

He sat down, then along came George and Thelma.
With relief, he noticed they did not seem out of sorts.
Still, when the plates were set in front of them, no plate
was placed in front of Gladys's chair.

"Wait!" Wally grunted as the young server turned to
leave. Before he could ask about Gladys, there she was,
making her way toward him, her coat on, an overnight
bag on her arm, and a sad look on her face.

She put a warm hand on his shoulder. He placed his
hand on top of hers to get more warmth from her.

"I'm sorry Wally. There's a storm coming and my son

wanted to come get me tonight before it hits." She looked near tears.

He struggled to his feet and went against his nature and in front of everyone hugged her. "It'll be all right. When are you coming back?"

"Sometime tomorrow, depending on the roads. It could be late." Her forehead wrinkled with worry and he reached out to smooth it.

"Well, then we'll see each other tomorrow night."

She smiled, returned the hug and not for the first time he realized that, although she only came up to his chin, now strong she was.

He could not sleep that night, but sat alone watching the storm, as if he could will it not to be too bad.

His daughter and her husband and their two teenage children surprised him by showing up to eat Christmas dinner with him. When he asked how the roads were, they said bad enough, but that her brother and his family and grand-child would be there sometime soon.

They finished eating and returned to his room and had to wait an hour before the others arrived and the time passed slowly with intermittent chatter while the teens kept busy on their phones. Wally realized staying longer was not fun for any of them.

Then the others arrived, and all eleven of them managed to squeeze into his room. The two teens sat on the windowsill, four adults on his bed, he held his great-grandson on his lap in his recliner, and the others stood around. This year, they had decided to do the Secret Santa thing to make the gift exchange a lot easier.

Before his daughter opened the bag of gifts, a knock came on his door.

Gladys's grin was wide as she stuck her head around the door, then she sobered. "Oh, I'm sorry."

"Wait!" Wally struggled to his feet, almost forgetting

to hand off the tot. "I'd like you to meet my family."

But Gladys was already backing out. "Another time perhaps. I just wanted to let you know I am back. "

Then she was gone.

"She seems nice," his daughter said.

"She is."

"Let's do the exchange, then we'll head out," she said, as if she knew he hadn't been able to give Gladys her gift yet.

"No rush," Wally said. "You can stay."

But for just a little while, he thought.

NOT ONCE BUT TWICE

In a room just off the library lobby, a writer's guild consisting of five people sit around a table, two empty chairs interspersed among them. Sadness infiltrates the reigning silence.

Bill clears his throat. "Shall we begin?"

At that moment, Elsie blows through the door and slams her briefcase down in front of one of the empty chairs. "Sorry, sorry. Bloody car wouldn't start, then I couldn't find Fred's keys to his car."

She flings her coat over the back of the chair then plunks her ample form into it. She briskly rubs her hands together. "Did everyone have a good Christmas?" Her usually animated features freeze as she takes in the somber expressions of the others. "What?"

Mary reaches over and pats Elsie's hand. "Didn't you hear, dear?"

"Hear what?" Elsie glances from Mary to each of the others, her eyes finally coming to rest upon the empty chair across from her. "Where's Doris?"

The pat turns into a squeeze. "She passed away, Elsie.

On Dec. 31."

"Cancer," Nora murmurs, shaking her head. "She was diagnosed in November, but swore me to secrecy."

Bill again clears his throat. "I emailed everyone of the news last week asking each of you to bring a copy of the email Doris sent out before Christmas." He sighs and adds, "So we could read it aloud here. One last critique for Doris, so to speak."

"Well, I didn't get any of the emails!" Elsie's voice has tightened into a raspy squeak. "My bloody computer died the second week of December right after our last meeting. I didn't even know . . . oh bloody Christ!"

For once, no one chides her for swearing.

Elsie sniffs. "What about a funeral? Did I miss that as well?"

"No," Bill says. "Her family chose to have a private ceremony. Which is why we are dedicating this meeting to Doris." He hands Elsie a sheet of paper. "Here's an extra copy of her last email." He scans the table. "Who would like to read?"

Everyone avoids looking at everyone else. Finally, Peter says, "You do it Bill, you're our leader, after all."

After an almost imperceptible nod, Bill clears his throat and begins in his no-nonsense voice.

To my wonderful writing group.

My apologies for not being able to attend the Christmas meeting, but here is my written contribution. I ask that you read it not once, but twice. Once to yourselves at home, and as a group at the next meeting.

I would like to begin my article with a question that mirrors the one Virginia asked Francis Church in the New York Sun in 1897. "Is there a Santa Claus?" Well the question I would like to put to you all is: "Is there such a thing as a ghost?"

My answer, like Church's, would be "a resounding yes." Now there are those that do not believe in anything they cannot see. As Mr. Church said, "There is a veil covering the unseen world which not the strongest man . . . could tear apart. Only faith, fancy, poetry, love, romance, can push aside that curtain and view the supernatural beauty and glory beyond."

Personally, I have not experienced anything that would indicate there is a realm beyond this world, but I have several friends who have.

There's Marilyn, who was driving along the coast when a sheep ran across the road in front of her. She braked and avoided hitting the poor thing and hadn't yet got up to speed when she rounded a corner to find the road ahead flooded out. If not for the sheep, she swears she would have been washed into the North Atlantic. She avers it was a guardian angel who spooked the sheep into running in front of her.

Carla now, while attending a family reunion at a cousin's large property outside of Halifax, lost one of her late mother's earrings that she saved for only the most special of occasions. She hadn't even noticed it'd fallen off until she got home and though her cousin searched high and low, the earring was nowhere to be found. At a similar gathering the following summer, Carla was out admiring the grounds when a crow squawked and squawked at her from the edge of the woods. Intent on putting an end to the annoying racket, Carla waved her arms and shouted. But the brazen black bird refused to move and instead squawked only louder. Carla stooped to pick up a rock and there, on the ground in front of her, lay the missing earring. At that very moment, the crow flew off and was not heard from again, at least not while Carla was there. Carla thought her mom used the crow to help her find the earring. Who can say definitely whether she was right or wrong?

Then there's Truman who went backpacking on a trail in Cape Breton. In the middle of the night, though he slept without disruption, his hiking mate swore he saw a man wearing a kilt and carrying a fish walk right through the fire and disappear into the woods. Research, of which Truman is fond of, revealed that Scottish immigrants had settled in the area.

Then there's Bob, a former Scouts leader, who told me of the time he led a troop on a hike in Kejimkujik. Though mid-day, a strange fog settled upon the forest, so dense they soon lost their way. The lad in charge of the compass admitted he'd inadvertently left it back at camp. They thought they should wait a bit, but the fog grew even denser as the forest around them stilled with an eerie silence. Then, the faint honk of a goose greeted them. First it would draw close, then retreat. When they moved toward it, it drifted away, always in the same direction. They continued to follow the sound and eventually they came upon the campground. When they mentioned the goose to the other campers, not a one had heard a single honk. Divine avian assistance? Perhaps.

And I must tell you about my dear friend Colleen. She awoke one morning smelling cedar. That day, she travelled to her aunt's funeral and stayed to help the family sort out her aunt's belongings. Upstairs, inside the closet, she came across a cedar chest. Inside she found her aunt's diary that detailed adventures her aunt had shared with Colleen's mother. By reading about the above exploits, she got a three dimensional glimpse of the person her mother had been. Would Colleen have even ventured to look into the chest had she not smelled cedar when she awoke that morning? I think not.

There's Bruce. He loved his animals. They were his family. The day his oldest cat Missy went missing, he searched the neighbourhood high and low. He was about to return home when he heard a dog barking. A big dog, from the sound of it, and strangely, it sounded exactly like the dog he had grown up with, a Saint Bernard named Sid. Well, he followed the sound to the back of a store. The moment he turned the corner, the barking ceased, but he heard something else: a sickly mewl coming from beneath an overturned crate. Sure enough, it was a weak and hungry Missy whose curiosity had nearly killed her. Bruce swears it was Sid who helped him find Missy.

Nancy, now, claims to hear a whisper that proves soothing whenever she gets in one of her snits. She is a cheerful sort most of the time, but her closest friends, me being one of them, know that at times she gets her knickers in a knot. Nancy thinks this whisper originates from beyond the threshold of the living to help her cope with life's rocky road.

And so, my friends. I believe there is something beyond this physical realm and that Dickens got it right, that spirits from beyond can extend an ethereal hand to help us struggling mortals.

I wish you all the Merriest of Christmases and may you be blessed with many hauntings.

Now make sure you read this, NOT ONCE. BUT TWICE.

Love Doris.

Sniffles, some suppressed, some not, trickle through the silence that has returned to the room.

Bill pushes his glasses up on his nose and after clearing his throat yet again, says, "Shall we begin our critique?"

"One bloody minute!" Elsie says. "She told us to read it twice and I've only had one go-around!" She holds the page in front of her, her eyes pouncing on every word. Once she has reached the bottom, she looks up. "Well, she stuck to her genre, paranormal fiction."

"But this sounds more like non-fiction," Mary says in her quiet voice. "She speaks of these friends as if they really exist. As if what they experienced actually happened."

"It doesn't really matter, does it?" Nora asks. "In the end, we all believe what we want to believe."

Elsie blows her nose with deliberation. "Wonder why she wanted us to read it twice? Maybe to just boss us about one last time, the twit." A pause, then, "I'll miss her, I will."

Then the overhead florescent lights flicker.

Not once.

But twice.

CAOL ÁIT

Creepy, Ted thought, as the calm sea in front of him nuzzled the rocky shore. Tendrils of fog curled heavenward like lost souls rising out of the sea. Still, the vista was a welcome respite compared to the pain riding in his son's eyes back at the house.

"Oh my God!"

The expletive startled Ted, and he whirled around. A woman stood there, looking at him. No, he decided, she seemed to be looking *through* him. Then her gaze shifted slightly, and her mouth emitted a piercing scream, the kind one would expect to hear in a B horror movie, not on an isolated beach in Cape Breton.

Fearful she did see ghosts rising out of the ocean, Ted wheeled around. The jerky movement threw him off balance, and he tripped over a protruding rock. His outstretched hands protected his face, but his left knee abutted a large slab, its smooth surface as unforgiving as concrete. He rolled back onto his rump and scanned the seas, but saw nothing unnatural. Still, his scalp prickled.

The woman rushed to his side and knelt beside him, at the last minute discarding what looked like a cigarette.

"Oh Lord, are you all right?"

Clutching his throbbing knee, he asked, "Why did you scream?"

Her eyebrows arched and she leaned back a bit. "You scared the bejesus out of me! It was like you came out of nowhere."

How could she have not seen him? But he asked what he considered to be the more important question: "What the hell were you looking at?"

She hesitated. "Oh, just the water." She tucked a lock of salt and pepper hair behind her ear. That, and the visible lines around her eyes led him to guess she was in her early fifties.

"Let me see your knee," she said. Without permission, she rolled up his pant leg. A lump had already formed on his boney knee. She touched it.

"Ouch!" He yanked his knee away.

"Ooh, I hope you didn't break your patella."

"My what?" He knew he sounded irritated, but damn it, he had reason to be.

"Your kneecap."

He rolled onto his hands, both of which felt as bruised as his ego, and, using his good knee, stood up. He wobbled as he tried to keep all the weight off his left leg. Without asking if she could help, she grabbed one of his elbows.

"I'm fine," he growled, and yanked his arm away. This motion caused him to shift weight onto his left. A sharp pain shot up his thigh and he would have fallen if the woman hadn't caught him. Although nearly a foot shorter than he, she managed to hold him up.

"Let's see if we can get you back to the house."

What house? The only house in the near vicinity was his son's.

Smiling somberly, she said, "You're Ted, Josh's dad,

right? I'm Elsie MacLeod, a friend of Marg's."

Marg. Josh's mother-in-law. She and her husband, George, were to arrive that afternoon. Ted hadn't expected them to bring someone else, a virtual stranger. Not at Christmas.

An awkward thought pulsed through him. Were they trying to set him up? He was nowhere near ready. It felt like Catherine had died just yesterday . . . he pushed aside unwanted images and focused on the current cause of ire: the last two times Marg and George had visited him in Toronto they had pestered him to start dating. If he learned this was their attempt at playing cupid, he would pack his bags and be gone before they could say 'humbug' . . . he paused in his thoughts as he realized this Elsie person was studying him, her alert grey eyes appearing to see right inside his head.

He expected her to say something, but she only smiled, a little too knowingly, and draped one of his arms over her shoulders, a little too casually.

In spite of her earlier exhibited strength, he knew that if he fell on her, he would likely kill her so he tried to walk without leaning on her too much.

"Come on!" she said, in a bossy tone. "I won't break. I'm actually more fit than I look."

She looked fit enough. A little on the heavy side, though that could be due to the bulky jacket she wore, but she moved with confidence. He tried another step, and had to wince.

"Christ, use me!" she said, then a giggle erupted from her lips, so sudden and sharp, it caught him by surprise.

"What's so funny?" His sense of humor had soured of late and at the moment it was non-existent.

She waved her free arm. "Nothing. My choice of words . . . oh, don't mind me." Another giggle, a softer one.

Was she flirting with him? This made him even more uncomfortable.

She must have sensed this, as she leaned away and spoke in a more gentle tone. "Want me to go fetch Josh?"

In the two years since that fatal accident Ted had only seen his son once, last summer when Josh and and his wife Diane had come to Toronto for a teachers' conference. That brief visit proved more intolerable than the obligatory phone conversations on birthdays and holidays. Awkward, forced conversation had replaced what had, before they'd lost Catherine, been easy, amiable chatter. When they were face to face, he could hardly look Josh in the eye, as the pain riding there seemed to meld with what he felt inside, feeding on it until he felt his chest would explode.

So no, he did not want her to fetch Josh. He shook his head and leaned on her for the next step. He immediately discovered this little bit of support helped immensely. In fact, with each step the throb subsided a little.

Elsie kept a slow pace, picking a path among the larger rocks until they reached the narrow dirt road that led back up to the house.

"You know," she began, and Ted wished she would remain silent. He didn't want to know, or get to know. The last thing he needed was some strange woman looking for romance.

Elsie continued. "Marg had no idea you were going to be here. She knew Diane had invited you but she didn't really expect you to come, as you didn't last Christmas. I've had a bit of a tough year, and Marg, being the good friend she is, talked me into coming." She stopped and peered up at him with those alert eyes. "Look, I understand if you're uncomfortable with my presence. Diane and Josh looked uneasy too when I showed up, as much as they tried to hide it. I think they're worried Marg and George are trying to hook us up."

Ted could not prevent a grunt from escaping. Then he feared he had offended her, but she laughed. Another loud bark, close to a snort.

He still didn't see the humor in the situation and was about to say so when she said, "C'mon, be real. As if a hunk like you would be interested in dumpy ol' me."

Hunk? He hadn't considered himself in that market since high school. Still, it was kinda nice to get a compliment, in spite of the situation. He grunted again. "You're too kind . . . and most likely near-sighted."

Another laugh snorted out of her. She covered her mouth. "Excuse me, I don't usually laugh this loud. Or talk this much. I'm rather shy . . . really," she added, after looking at the disbelief he knew was registered on his face.

She giggled some more. "But don't worry," she went on, "I'm not about to make any moves on you. Besides, you probably have some young thing up in Toronto waiting for you."

Her eastern roots showed with her reference to Toronto as 'up'.

"No, I don't." He responded, then regretted his words. He didn't want her to think he was in the market for anyone, young or otherwise.

"Well I have to tell ya that, even though you wouldn't notice me midst a pack of penguins, if I *was* so inclined, I would probably make a move for you. But don't worry," she added hastily, "I'm not so inclined."

A sliver of disappointment surprised him. She must have recognized him as damaged goods. And rightly so.

"I see."

"No, I don't think you do," she said, a smile still tugging at the corners of her mouth.

After a few more steps, she said. "I'm gay."

He halted. Before he could think of something to say, she pulled him back into motion.

"Marg knows," she said. "George doesn't though, and Marg and I would rather he didn't. He's a dear, but definitely old school in a redneck kind of way, and I don't want to risk losing the fun I have with him and Marg. My friends back in Halifax all know, but it's different with people from smaller towns. They think differently, and Christ, what the hell am I telling you all this for?"

Ted felt both honored and more than a little relieved. "I won't say a word," He said softly, and with the arm he had draped over her shoulder, gave her a gentle squeeze. She smiled up at him then, a warm, grateful smile that softened her features.

"And I would too be able to tell you from a pack of penguins," he added.

"Hah!" she laughed, a guffaw so deep it could have originated from a large man. "You're too kind," she said, then added, "and likely near-sighted too." She giggled anew, and Lou found himself laughing with her.

The trees lining the road soaked up the sound of the sea, and though a mist hovered here and there, Ted did not find it nearly so spooky. Or was it just Elsie's calming presence? In the space of just a few minutes, she had gone from being an intrusion to someone he could consider a friend.

They turned a corner and the house with its large, landscaped backyard came into view. Seconds later, Josh came running out. "What happened?" His voice sounded tight.

Though Josh had Ted's dark coloring and build, his worried expression reminded Ted of Catherine and that inner ache, never far from the surface, returned with full force and he had to look away. If he didn't know better, he would have thought he was having a heart attack.

Anger? Grief? No, he decided, it was more like standing at the edge of a cliff with an ever-strengthening wind threatening to blow you over. He bent down to look at his knee.

"Tripped and hit my knee. It's not too bad, really." Through his pant leg he could tell the joint had nearly doubled in size and felt spongy to the touch. But it wasn't that sore. Nothing compared to what he felt inside.

He let go of Elsie and tested his leg. "See? I'm fine." Leaning on the rail, he managed to navigate the three steps onto the deck. Elsie pushed the patio door open and gave him a look as he passed by that said she knew he was anything but fine.

As Josh went into the kitchen for ice, Marg, George, and Diane all rushed over the moment they spotted Ted limping.

Ted relaxed down into a chair and Diane found him a stool to rest his leg on.

"It's a good thing Elsie found you," Marg said.

"Oh, I found him all right," Elsie said, her eyes twinkling. Whether she was oblivious to the tension in the air, or she was intentionally trying to dispel it, Ted didn't care.

"Yeah," He pretended to grumble. "She scared the shit out of me!"

Elsie dismissed his words with an exaggerated wave. "Now don't go blaming this on me. You startled me first, remember?"

It had been a long time since Ted had been teased, particularly with no strings attached, and he entered the fray with enthusiasm. "How could I scare YOU? You snuck up on ME."

"I had no idea you were there!"

"But I was right in front of you."

Elsie grunted and gestured the length of him. "Yeah,

right. Gray pants. Gray coat. Gray hair. Standing on gray rocks against a gray sea and sky. If you hadn't moved, I never would have seen you. "

Ted wanted the banter to continue. "Well, you are a bit near-sighted."

Her infectious laugh made him join in, as well as the others, including Josh who arrived with a bag of frozen peas for Ted's knee, though by the look on their faces, they really didn't get it, which made Ted and Elsie laugh harder.

Ted caught Josh's gaze and his son's smile froze into insincerity as his eyes dulled. Ted looked away and sighed. Would he ever be able to laugh with his son again?

Josh excused himself to go wrap presents while the women headed toward the kitchen. George followed with a promise to return with a beer.

While Ted adjusted the bag on his knee, his thoughts returned to the beach, and Elsie's distant look before she spotted him. Those eyes of hers had seen more than just the beach, he was certain of it. Later, he thought. He would make a point of asking her later.

* * *

Wearing the sweater Josh and Diane had given him the previous Christmas, that first Christmas without Catherine, Ted exited the den which he'd taken as his bedroom, using the blow-up bed Diane and Josh had bought during their 'apartment years'. Elsie had wanted him to take his designated bedroom upstairs, but when he said the stairs would be hard on his knee, she had relinquished her stand, something, he guessed, she was not used to doing. He hoped her humor would provide a buffer that would allow him to make it through the evening. He planned to retire early and leave the next day the moment the presents were opened. Do his duty, so to speak. Let Josh enjoy what was left of Christmas.

As he entered the 'great room' he saw Diane staring out the window. Chatter and giggles came from the dining room around the corner, a contrast to the frown he noticed creasing Diane's young forehead.

Ted had cared for this young woman from the moment Josh had brought her home during their junior year at Waterloo. When things became serious, Ted and Catherine had been drawn into Diane's large, boisterous family, and although the Vincents lived in Nova Scotia, the in-laws became close friends, and flew often to Toronto to 'hang out' with he and Catherine. Until the accident, that is.

He focused on his daughter-in-law. "Everything okay?"

She turned from the window, her frown disappearing above a warm smile. Her dimples seemed deeper. She was not so thin, either. Returning home to the East Coast obviously suited her. She would age into her mother's twin, Ted thought, which wasn't a bad thing. Marg's tall frame had thickened slightly at the waist, but her fine features had hardly aged in the six years he had known her, and she always dressed impeccably in contrast to her forever wrinkled husband, with his angular nose and hair that, although thinning and trimmed very short, appeared to constantly rebel against all taming efforts.

Diane pointed out the window. "I was hoping for a white Christmas."

Ted limped over and peered out. The deck lights failed to penetrate the thick fog that now surrounded the house. A few dark shapes were discernible, which he guessed to be trees. But one couldn't be sure. The hairs on his neck, still damp from his shower, began to lift. He glanced quickly at Diane, but her smile persisted as she studied the yard.

"We had snow at Halloween, for God's sakes, drifts of it, and it was miserably cold. I figured at least some of it would last until Christmas. Then we had that horrible rain that washed it all away. Even though it's supposed to turn cold, there's no snow in the forecast until January. But enough griping." She turned back to him with a grin below large eyes that let her warm soul shine through and, not for the first time, Ted suspected it was this that had first drawn Josh to her.

She threaded her arm through his. "Come on, dinner's on the table. I'm so glad you decided to come, Ted."

He knew Diane liked a crowd, especially at Christmas. Until this year, she and all her siblings had gathered at the Vincents' home in Truro for Christmas. However, two of her siblings had recently moved out west, and the two living in Halifax with toddlers wanted to begin their own traditions, so Marg and George decided to spend Christmas with Diane and Josh in their new home in Cape Breton.

"Thanks for being so persistent in inviting me," Ted answered, and meant it. He decided to try to keep his mood light and enjoy the evening. Perhaps tease Elsie. Surely he could do that. Catherine would want him to. She would also want him to hug Josh.

Ted jerked to a stop. The latter idea had seemed to pop into his head on its own, as if from an external source.

"You okay?" Diane asked. "Is it your knee?"

"No, I'm fine." Just going a little crazy, he added to himself. He, Josh, and Catherine, had always been a 'huggy' family, mainly due to Catherine's influence. He and Josh's hugs had waned over the years, particularly after Josh left for university. But since the accident, they had become non-existent.

When they entered the dining room, Elsie lifted her wine glass to Ted. He waved back, and caught a quick glance between Diane and Josh, a rather worried look, and he decided perhaps he should ask Elsie if he could let them in on her little secret.

Josh held up an open bottle of wine. "Red, right?" A direct gaze this time.

Ted held it until the ache began, then, with a smile he hoped looked authentic, lifted his glass. "Please."

"Good," Elsie said. "More white for us ladies."

"Elsie, dearie, you are such a bad influence," Marg said. "You're liable to have me drunk and in-bed long before Santa comes."

"Oh, pooh!" Elsie said. "It's Christmas eve. Tomorrow you can sleep as late as you want."

"Not on Christmas morning!" Diane wailed.

Josh laughed. "You see, Elsie, my wife gets more excited this time of year than most children do. Their fault." He pointed to Marg and George. "Even after we were married, they would make us wait at the top of the stairs along with all Di's sibs and their spouses and not come down until they had everything all ready. Then, instead of five children tromping down the steps, they had a stampede of giddy adults."

Ted grinned. After Josh and Diane got married, Ed and Marg had allowed him and Catherine to help with the preparations: stuffing the gigantic stockings to overflowing, placing all the presents beneath the tree, arranging various candies, fruits, and baked goods about the room. Marg hadn't worked outside the home, and raising five children on George's teacher's salary had been difficult at times, Ted guessed, but they had always managed to set enough aside to make Christmas feel like a bonanza. Catherine had jumped into the fray with the enthusiasm of a child herself. A heavy, too familiar sadness swept over him.

Elsie leaned over the table. "How's the leg, Chester?" With that simple act, she managed to pull him back from the cliff, and he was grateful for it. He answered, "Just fine, Mrs. Dillon, just fine."

Marg and George laughed, but Josh and Diane looked puzzled.

"From a television show, me dears," Elsie explained. "Long before you were born."

"Oh, I thought you were referring to one of your characters," Diane said.

"Characters?" Ted asked.

"Elsie's a famous author," Marg said, pride instilling a smugness in her smile.

"Infamous maybe," Elsie said, "and only around the Halifax harbor bars."

"You've published your what, your sixth novel?" Marg said. "And didn't you tell me they're waiting for the manuscript for the next one?"

Elsie grimaced. "And they'll be waiting a while yet." She looked up at Ted. "I've hit a bit of a stall."

"Six? Wow. What kind of novels?" Ted asked.

"Ghost stories," she responded.

That prickly feeling returned again. Elsie narrowed her eyes and looked about to ask him an unanswerable question when Diane urged everyone to dig into their spaghetti before it got cold.

After a few mouthfuls, George said to Elsie, "Those editors should give you some space."

Marg elbowed George, as if to keep him quiet.

Diane, who was sitting next to Ted, reached across the table and squeezed Elsie's hand. "Marg told me about your friend, Elsie. I'm so sorry."

Ted looked questionably at George, who waved his half-eaten roll as he responded, "Her roommate, Joanne. Just finished a half-marathon last spring when she dropped dead."

Marg threw her husband a glare that held daggers.

"What?" George said. "Ted didn't know. Probably easier for me to tell him, right, Elsie?"

Elsie waved at Marg. "It's okay. I'm coming to terms with it. Aren't I, Jo?" She raised her glass to the ceiling, took a long swallow, then beamed around the table.

Ted suppressed an urge to look in the same direction, in case his burgeoning imagination actually saw something.

"Come on, folks," Elsie spoke into the ensuing silence. "It's Christmas, and we're with friends, family, good food and drink. Things could not be better!" She raised her glass in another toast and did not lower it until everyone joined her with a clink and a sip.

They all attacked their plates and just when Ted felt the atmosphere begin to grow taut, once more, Elsie spoke up. "So, Josh. How do you like teaching at the college?"

"You mean, the University of Cape Breton," Diane corrected.

"Oh, excuse me," Elsie said with a laugh. "I forgot."

Josh grinned at Elsie. "I'm enjoying it. With the expansion, I might even get tenure in a couple of years."

Ted had been surprised when Josh had taken the teaching job. He had expected his son to go into management in industry, as he had done. But Josh wanted to teach computer science and live in Nova Scotia. Not long after they moved to Sydney, Diane procured a job at an elementary school and they were able to purchase this home.

"Hey, pass down more of that spaghetti," Elsie said. "It's delicious, Diane."

"Oh, Josh made it. It's Ted's recipe, really."

Elsie raised her eyebrows at Ted. "Ooh, a hunk, and he can cook, too."

Ted felt himself blushing. Before the Vincents came on the scene, many a Christmas Eve had been spent making meatballs. Another ache coursed through him but it was abruptly cut off by George giving Marg a nudge. That, combined with a wink from Elsie and it was all Ted could do not to laugh aloud.

When everyone took a rain check on dessert, Diane stood up and spoke in the tone of a seasoned emcee. "Ladies and gentlemen, it is my supreme pleasure to announce a new Christmas tradition." After the nominal pause, she said, "Henceforth, every Christmas Eve, we'll have Ted's spaghetti and meatballs, after which the men-folk shall clean up while the women sip wine by the fire."

"Here, here," Elsie said, taking another sip and refilling her glass. She plucked the bottle from the table. "Follow me, woman-folk."

As Ted struggled to get out of the chair, she said to him, "You going to be able to manage, Chester?"

"It's just a little stiff."

Josh took the plate Ted had picked up. "You can supervise, Dad."

At that moment, Ted had an overwhelming urge to reach out and pull his son to him. But alarmed at the moisture he felt filling his eyes, he turned toward the kitchen and said, "Oh, I like supervising." His attempt at levity failed, he knew, by the edge he heard in his own voice and by the barely audible sigh behind him.

"I just have one question," George said as he placed the stack of plates onto the counter. "Why do we need a new tradition? I liked the old ones just fine."

Ted leaned against the counter and proceeded to instruct George on the proper technique of placing the dishes in the dishwasher until George told him exactly where he'd like to put the dishes, especially the forks.

Josh tackled the pans at the sink. Lou noticed the tension in his son's shoulders. He limped over and picked up a dishtowel.

"You don't have to do that," Josh said out of the side of his mouth.

"Oh, let him," George growled good-naturedly. "He's a poor lookin' ornament. Besides the sooner we get this done, the sooner I can light my cigar. It doesn't taste nearly as good if the flavor of the food has left your mouth."

"Uh, George?" Josh said tentatively. "Diane also has a new rule. No smoking inside." He looked apologetic. "Sorry, but she wants you to quit anyway."

In spite of a sharp look, George remained quiet. As soon as the kitchen was clean, he went to the coat rack by the door and pulled down his coat.

Ted reached for his as well. "I'll join you."

"Hey," Elsie said, hopping up from the great room onto the landing. "Wait for me."

George blinked at her. "You said you quit smoking."

"I have," she said, and pulled on her coat.

Ted remembered the cigarette at the beach and frowned at her.

She grinned and added. "Cigarettes, that is." She patted her coat pocket.

Marg leapt to her feet. "Don't tell me you brought contraband with you on the plane."

"No, silly," Elsie said. "I stuffed it into an empty bottle of Geratol and packed it in my suitcase. I did some rolling while I was waiting for you to get your face on for supper."

Marg planted her hands on her hips and towered over her shorter friend. "You could have been arrested! That stuff is illegal, you know."

Elsie giggled and stepped toward the door. "You coming?"

"Damn right I am!" Marg said, and reached for her coat.

Josh built up a fire in the pit in the middle of the yard while the rest of them brought chairs down off the deck. No wind stirred the thick fog and the leaping flames provided a large circle of warmth.

Then why the chill running down my spine? Ted wondered, refusing to look into the dense, wet darkness about them.

As George lit his second cigar, he looked at Ted. "Sure you don't want one of these?"

"No, thanks." Catherine had cured him of both cigarettes and cigars many years before.

"Want some of this?" Elsie held out a small remnant of a joint.

Ted looked at it a moment, then reached for it. He took his time inhaling, afraid the now unfamiliar smoke would make him cough. But it didn't, and he let it out slowly.

"Hey, Dad, you almost look like you know what you're doing," Josh said, and his grin looked real.

Pride-tinged joy tickled Ted. "Actually, I've never had marijuana before."

Elsie stared at him. "Really?"

Marg gave Elsie a dig in the ribs. "Here, hand it over." After she took an extended drag, to the oohs and ahhs of the others, she handed it toward Diane. Diane shook her head.

"Really? What about you, Josh?"

"No, I had too much wine with supper." He put his

arm around Diane and gave her a squeeze. "Besides, Di's going to make me get up early tomorrow."

Diane shook her finger at the rest of them. "You all have to get up early. No matter how fuzzy in the head you get tonight."

Elsie let smoke leak out her nose. "Though I'm not usually a morning person, I'll be as clear as a bell because, man, am I going to sleep good tonight after all that great food and wine."

"Look at how thick this fog has gotten," Josh said, peering around. "You can't even see the end of the property."

Creepy, Ted thought.

As if to contradict his thoughts, Elsie said, "It's so beautiful here, Josh. How did you find it?"

"Luck. It had just come on the market when we started looking. The previous owners decided to move into a seniors' apartment in town. Most of the land around here has been sold to a developer, but the lots will be at least three acres in size. We own five acres ourselves, so we won't lose any privacy."

"It is special," Elsie said, as if she knew something. She handed Ted a newly lit joint.

Ted inhaled deeply and the effect loosened his tongue. "So tell me," he said as he handed her back the joint. "Just what did you find so special down at the beach?"

Elsie raised her eyebrows. "Pardon me?"

"You were looking at something other than me. You said, 'Oh my God,' or something like that."

George grunted. "Well, you are a hunk."

Marg slapped George's arm, Dianne and Josh exchanged another concerned glance, and Elsie snorted.

This didn't bother Ted. What did bother him was whatever Elsie had seen. "Before you knew I was there, what were you looking at?"

Elsie exhaled what smoke remained in her lungs, and said, "Caol Áit."

The others chorused, "What?"

"Caol Áit. It's Gaelic. It means 'a thin place'." She pointed in the direction of the ocean. "What you have down at the beach is a thin place."

For a moment no one spoke. Ted wasn't sure he even wanted to know what a thin place was. Something eerie, no doubt.

George broke the silence. "Okay, I'll bite. What's a thin place?"

Elsie stared into the flames as she spoke, her voice calm, almost reverential. "According to Celtic tradition, a thin place is where this world and the spirit world come close together. The veil between the two worlds becomes 'thin'."

Marg shook her shoulders. "Sounds creepy."

Thank-you, Ted thought.

Marg pointed a finger at her friend. "If your dope makes me paranoid and gives me scary dreams tonight, I'm going wake you up in the rudest of fashions."

Elsie smiled "It's not scary. Quite the opposite, right, kids?"

Both Josh and Diane nodded.

Ted shivered, and to make it look like he was cold, pulled the zipper on his jacket up to his neck and leaned toward the flames. No one else seemed to notice. No one except Elsie. He decided to challenge her knowing look.

"You didn't answer my question. Just what did you see in this thin place?"

"Nothing. I just felt, I don't know, a closeness. To what, or whom, I didn't get a chance to find out. You moved, and startled me. You know, if it wasn't so dark and foggy, and I wasn't so high, I'd go there right now."

"And do what?"

"Just sit and wait."

George spoke before Ted could. "For what?"

Elsie shrugged. "For that feeling of closeness, if nothing else."

In spite of the marijuana, Ted found himself getting cross. "Closeness to what? Are you saying you expect to see a ghost or something?"

Elsie smiled, obviously unperturbed by his tone. "Something."

Josh stood up and reached for more wood, but Elsie stopped him with a hand on his arm. "Time for dessert, my dear."

Knowing they would get nothing further from Elsie, and because he did feel a bit hungry in spite his two helpings of spaghetti, Ted agreed with her. Before they entered the house he shivered again, only this time it was from the cold.

"Brrr," Diane said. "The temperature is dropping."

Diane made them a pot of tea, something Lou hadn't had much of before Josh and she hooked up, to go with her pineapple cheesecake. Although Ted wasn't one for sweets, he found this dessert absolutely delicious. With all of them going at it, soon only one solitary piece remained in the dish.

As the others took their plates to the sink, Elsie placed the dish on the table between her and Ted. She waved her fork. "Can't leave this sitting here alone all night. Help me finish it up, will ya?"

Ted picked up the fork he had just set down.

Diane yawned, then said. "Leave the dishes until the morning. And no-one, I repeat, no-one comes down the stairs until Josh and I say so." She jabbed a finger at Ted. "And you stay in the den until we say it's safe to come out. Savvy?"

His mouth full, Ted only nodded.

Marg herded George toward the stairs behind Josh and Diane. "Come on, mister. Warm the bed up while I brush my teeth."

George winked at Lou over his shoulder. "Don't stay up too late, kids."

As they turned the corner, Marg cast a worried glance back down at them.

Elsie swallowed a forkful, then giggled. "You know, we could have some real fun with George." She laughed. "Poor George. I nearly told him at Jo's funeral. Then I decided it wasn't really important. Marg worries about him knowing more than I do."

Ted felt a bond had formed between them, and not just from their mutual enjoyment of the cheesecake. "When did Jo . . . ?" He found he could not say the word 'die'.

"Last March."

So recently? Ted thought. "Were you together long?"

"Officially, we'd been living together almost three years. Unofficially, we'd been seeing each other exclusively for nearly twenty."

Ted and Catherine had been married just over thirty years. Could grief be quantified in terms of time? To his chagrin, he noticed tears welling in Elsie's eyes.

"I'm sorry, I shouldn't have prodded."

She smiled warmly as two large drops tracked down her cheeks. "No, I appreciate being able to talk about her. She was a wonderful person, and I feel so blessed to have known her as long as I did."

In spite of the tears, Ted saw acceptance, even peace. Elsie absently gathered up the remnants of the graham cracker crust with a finger. "At first, I was sooooo pissed off. Then for a while, depressed. One day she told me to move on."

A chill iced Ted's spine. "She *told* you?"

"Not in so many words, actually, not in any words. She just . . ." Elsie paused, as if looking for the right way to explain it. She reached over and squeezed Ted's hand. "It was a feeling I got . . . at a thin place. Fundy Park in New Brunswick. We used to hike there all the time, and one summer day, I just packed a lunch and went on one of our favorite hikes by myself."

Ted swallowed past his tightening throat. "You saw her?"

"No." That quiet, knowing smile lingered on Elsie's lips. "But I kinda felt her. Then I started bawling. When I settled down, I gave her supreme shit for leaving me."

"And she answered?" Ted found himself leaning over the table, hanging on every word. What was he expecting? Proof of life after death?

Again, that smile. "Not really. But I could easily imagine how she would respond, and man, I got a talking to. As close as we were, we still had the odd spat. Snitty fits we used to call them."

"What did she say?"

Elsie wiped away another tear. "Move on. You're still alive, enjoy it." Elsie laughed, this time a soft, gentle, almost musical sound. "The voice in my head sure sounded like the ol' Jo."

Elsie's distant gaze refocused on Ted, and he found the scrutiny uncomfortable. He picked up the empty dish and started to get up. Elsie reached out pushed on his shoulder until he sat back down.

"So what's up with you and Josh?"

What's up? He felt like screaming, 'Catherine's dead, that's what!'.Instead he bit his lip and studied the crumbs on the table. He could feel Elsie's eyes on him.

"Need another joint?" she asked softly.

"No, thanks. I . . . I guess I'm still angry."

"At Josh?"

Startled, Lou looked up. "Heavens, no. Why would I be?"

"There's a wall between you two a ghost couldn't walk through."

Ted couldn't explain the wall, either to himself or her. "We're both still struggling, I guess."

"How did Catherine die?" Elsie prompted.

She must know from Marg, Ted thought. Besides, he didn't want to talk about it. Elsie squeezed his arm again. He looked up into eyes that held no judgment, no anger, just warmth.

He sighed, not sure if the words would come. Then, to his surprise, they tumbled out. "The weather was bad. Snow, sleet, freezing rain. The only thing that didn't change every half-mile was that cold wind out of the north. After she drove me to work, I told her to go right home, but no, she had to go to that damn volunteer job . . ." His throat threatened to close and Ted forced a swallow. "She made me quit smoking. Cut down on the drinking. She made me eat right, and exercise. All so we could do everything we wanted to when I retired. Then dammit, she heads onto the 401, midst all that traffic and the icy roads . . ." Sobs rose in his throat. He had an irrepressible urge to flee. But Elsie still had a tight hold on his arm, and he knew it would be a real physical struggle to get free.

"It wasn't her idea to go so early." Elsie said gently. "Things happen beyond our control."

Ted glared at Elsie through tears he could not will away. "Oh, I suppose you're going to tell me about divine intervention, or some greater bullshit plan."

"No, I'm not. And you already know that she would not want you to spend the rest of your days angry and alone, so I'm not going to tell you that either."

"I have no intention of finding someone else."

"I wasn't talking about finding another love. I was talking about being apart from your son. Have you two even discussed Catherine's death?"

"No. It's too painful. As much for him as me. Even I can see that."

"Loss is painful. But not terminal. Life does go on. You and Josh have to realize that. Become a family once again."

"Without Catherine we have no family."

Elsie abruptly stood up and took the dish to the sink. Ted immediately missed her warm grip. "It's sad," she said over her shoulder as she ran water over the dishes. "In that one accident, Josh lost his mother, his father, and his family."

Ted lurched to his feet in anger. Hot tears now flowed copiously down his cheeks, but his anger overcame his humility. He pulled Elsie around to face him. "Just what the hell are we supposed to do? We can't just forget she ever existed."

"That's the last thing you should do!" Elsie's eyes flashed with heat. Even though she had to look up at him, Ted felt he was the one on the defensive. "Whether or not you believe a soul survives death, Catherine will never be gone as long as she lives in there." She stabbed a finger into his chest, hard enough to make him wince. "And in here." Then she tapped her own forehead, probably because she couldn't reach his. "All you have to do is talk to her, whether you think she's in heaven, or at the beach, or just inside you."

He covered his face with his hands. Elsie wrapped her arms about his chest and pulled him close. Her warm hug made him cry even harder, and he returned the hug.

Her voice softened. "Just talk to her, Ted. All you gotta do is listen."

Was it really that simple? He heard a creak on the

stairs, and pulled away, hastily wiping his face.

"Who was it?" he asked.

Elsie grinned. "I'm not sure, but I hope it was George."

Ted pulled out a handkerchief and blew his nose. "Maybe in the morning, we should tell him we're engaged."

Elsie snorted softly into her hand. "I'm off to bed before you make me laugh and wake everyone up. I suggest you do the same, or Santa won't come." Before he could say anything else, she went up the stairs.

Ted shut off the lights and stepped into the den. He lingered in the dark, thinking of Catherine.

Are you there? he asked. Are you really there? He begged for a sign. He had never accepted religion or its promises so he didn't believe in ghosts. Not really.

Just talk to her, Elsie had said. Well, if she were here, what would he say?

I miss you, were the first words that came to mind.

He listened.

But not a creature was stirring, from either world.

* * *

Ted sat up, uncertain as to what had awakened him. He had been thinking about something. No, he decided, it had been a dream. Only instead of images, there were words tumbling in his head. He squeezed his eyes shut tight, as if that would squeeze them back into his memory. *Don't look back* . . . or something like that. They had not been spoken by Catherine, for surely he would have remembered that. Who or what had said the words, he had no idea. *Don't look back.* Not bad advice, considering the circumstances.

A pale light stole through the curtains of the small window. The moment he stood up, his knee reminded him of the abuse he had inflicted upon it the day before. Carefully he dressed as fast as he could, as the furnace had not yet come on, another indication of how early it was. He paused at the door and listened. When all remained quiet, he opened the door and peeked out.

There were no presents beneath the huge Christmas tree and the stockings hung still empty, so he knew Mrs. Santa, aka Diane, wasn't up yet. Through the patio doors, the world remained a dark grey. Well, Catherine might not talk to him, and she might truly be gone but, like Elsie said, he could still talk to her. And what better place than the beach?

He hurriedly pulled on his coat and limped outside, soon discovering that his knee, like the day before, loosened up and hurt a little less with each step. He paused on the deck and blinked at the world around him.

A thin layer of ice coated everything. He'd heard of ice fog, but had never seen it, nor the effects of it, before. Along the road to the beach, each limb and branch gleamed with nature's silver gild. He'd have to wake Diane up when he got back, he thought. There may not be any snow, but the world couldn't look more Christmassy.

Before he stepped out onto the beach, he noticed the sea was still calm and a thin fog floated over the surface as it had the day before. But the vista before him no longer felt creepy.

He breathed deeply, tasting the salt in the air. At that moment, more words from his dream came to him. *Don't look back, I'm right beside you.* Nice words. He knew there were more words but his mind felt as fogged in as the ocean. But, as he hardly ever remembered dreams, it was remarkable he could recall this much

A plop to his right startled him. Josh squatted on a large rock that had been covered by the higher tide the previous afternoon. He selected another stone from a pile in his left hand and lobbed it softly out into the deeper water. The ensuing ripples dissipated quickly.

Ted deliberately crunched his shoes on the pebbles to announce his approach and Josh stood up.

"Careful," Josh called over to him. "It's quite slippery. Everything's coated with ice."

It was a little slippery. Ted's left knee protested so he took it slow. By the time he reached Josh, his son had returned his attention to the sea.

"You're not supposed to be out of your room," Josh said without turning his head.

"I didn't think anyone was up, so I thought I'd check out this *thin* place."

Josh breathed deeply. "I think Mom would have liked it here."

Ted tried to swallow the lump that suddenly formed in his throat. "I'm sure she would have."

Josh's rapid blinking told Ted that his son was desperately trying not to cry.

Ted laid a hand on his son's shoulders. To his surprise, Josh wheeled toward him, his features crumpling in pain. "Christ, Dad, I'm so sorry!"

Ted stood back in shock. "You're sorry? Whatever for?"

Josh struggled to get words out between his sobs and Ted was reminded of the time when Josh had wrecked his bicycle. "It . . it was my fault mom died!"

Ted blinked in disbelief. "Josh . . . Jesus Christ, Josh, you weren't even in the province when it happened!"

"The reason she had to drive you to work in the first

place was because I was using your SUV to move my stuff. If I . . . if . . ." Here, the sobs won out.

"Good God." Ted gathered his son into his arms. Josh latched onto Ted and sobbed hard into his shoulder. Ted's tears flowed too, and he didn't try to stop them. He felt a warmth, whether it was from the heat produced by their hug, or something else, he didn't know, and he didn't care. He wanted to comfort his son, ease his pain.

"Josh, it's just as much my fault. I should have insisted she not go to the hospital that day. Or I could have just made her stay home when I went to work." Ted realized then that they had both been harbouring feelings of guilt, and it was this, not anger that had kept them apart.

Josh leaned back. "Dad, that's ridiculous!"

Ted narrowed his eyes at his son. "No more than your theory." Then a thought came to him. "You know what your mother would say right now?"

Josh wiped his face, grinned and nodded. "Yeah. She'd tell us to agree to disagree and go back to the game."

Ted grinned. Josh had learned to play chess at the age of eight. As the years went by, their chatter over the board grew into animated debates, and Josh's response was an accurate rendition of what Catherine would have said. He even sounded like her just then.

Ted squeezed his son's shoulder. "So, shall we get back to the game?"

Before Josh could respond a squeal came from across the beach.

"Ooh, you are in such big trouble!" Diane jogged towards them. She slipped and almost fell.

"Jesus, Diane!," Josh shouted. "Watch it!" He raced to her side. "You could have fallen."

Josh's stern tone surprised Ted. When he reached them, he said, "She's not made of glass, Josh."

"No, but . . ." Diane cut Josh off with a playful punch

to his abdomen.

But what? Ted studied the two of them, their guilty glances reminding him of teenagers caught in the act of doing something forbidden. He recalled that Diane had only sipped her wine. And she had not smoked any of Elsie's 'stash'.

"Are you . . . ?" When their looks confirmed Ted's suspicion, joy flooded through him. He picked Diane up and hugged her, but not too tightly.

"Whoa, Dad," Josh said. "We're not totally certain. She hasn't even seen the doctor yet, so we weren't going to tell anyone. At least not for awhile."

"Did you take a home test?" Ted asked.

Diane nodded, her eyes bright.

"My God!" Ted swung back toward the ocean and shouted, "Did you hear that Catherine?"

Both Josh and Diane frowned in worry.

"It's okay," Ted said. "I'm not losing my marbles. Then, maybe I am." He grinned. "And I couldn't feel better!"

"Maybe you've been spending a little two much time with Elsie," Diane said.

"Speaking of Elsie," Josh began in a tentative voice, "I came down last night for a glass of water and I saw you two. Did you know . . ." he cleared his throat and began again, "did you know that she's . . ."

"Gay, I know."

Relief erased Josh's frown. "Don't get me wrong," he said. "I have no problem with you seeing someone . . . I just didn't want you to get hurt." Josh's eyes, so like the ones Ted saw in the mirror each morning, were filled with concern. Concern for him.

Although he no longer needed help to walk, Ted draped one arm over Josh and the other over Diane as they headed back to the house.

* * *

"Can I come out yet?" Ted called through the door.

"Don't let him out until we're at the bottom of the stairs," George bellowed from somewhere upstairs.

"Okay, Ted," Diane called, "Count to ten . . ." she stopped, as Ted was already in front of her.

He shrugged. "Sorry, I came out on 'okay'."

George thumped down the stairs ahead of the women. "No fair! You saw the room first."

"Oh, don't be such a whiny baby," Elsie chided as she and Marg joined them.

"Now stop bickering," Marg said, "all of you, or we might be banished back to our rooms."

A flurry of gift opening followed. Ted perched beside Josh and traded barbs across the room with George as they compared what they each got in their stocking. Elsie made a fuss of every gift, demonstrating to everyone how each item worked or how it fit or didn't fit. Ted found himself laughing so hard his ribs began to feel sore.

At the end, Diane handed Josh a small parcel. Thinking it was something personal, Ted stood up and headed for the kitchen. Time for another tradition: waffles. He was sure Diane wouldn't mind him whipping up a batch.

To his surprise, George followed him into the kitchen, leaned close, and whispered, "There's something you should know about Elsie."

Ted stared down at his friend and with an effort kept

his voice low. "You know she's gay?"

George put a finger to his lips. "Shh. I've suspected it for years. Then when she and Joanne shacked up . . .well, I can add two and two and get four." His eyes widened with conspiratorial solemnity. "But don't let on to Marg, . . . hey, what's so funny?"

It seemed as if all the laughs Ted had been suppressing for nearly two years were looking for any reason to spill out. He laughed so hard his side ached.

"Er, Dad?"

Josh stood nearby, holding what looked like a picture frame. His eyes brimmed with tears. Without a word, Josh handed it to Ted. It was not a picture, but a framed piece of paper with rough edges and a yellowed hue. Upon it were two sentences written in Catherine's tidy script.

Josh pointed to the frame. "Diane found that piece of paper when she was tidying up the spare rooms last week and had it framed. It's from a letter Mom had written to me at my first summer camp. I was so homesick, remember, Dad? The second day there, I called long distance to your work and asked you to come get me."

Ted nodded. "I wanted to, but your mother talked me out of it, saying it would be better if you stayed."

"It turned out to be the best time of my life and look at all the summer jobs I got working at that same camp."

Ted nodded. "Your mother had been right, as usual."

"Mom sent me a letter through priority mail. Her last two sentences convinced me to stay. I cut out those words, and kept them with me the whole time. I even took that piece of paper with me when I left for university."

Tears blurred Teds vision as he read and re-read the words in front of him, the very same words from his dream:

Don't look back, I'm right beside you.
Just look around, and I'll be there.

The End

NEW MEMORIES

Fred leaned over the steering wheel as if that would help him see the road better. The center line had long been obliterated by the heavy wet snow that had fallen in the last hour and he could only tell where the road was by the tracks of the few cars that had preceded him.

Dammit, Margaret, he grumbled to himself. Where the hell are you? When his sister Margaret had called to say her daughter had bought her the airline ticket to visit him over Christmas, Fred had asked her to get a cab from the airport. But she said she just simply couldn't afford it and couldn't he at least pick his only sister up at the airport?

But Margaret had not arrived on the arranged flight, and only after a long wait at the information counter had he learned she hadn't made that flight, nor was she booked on later ones. As he didn't own a cell phone, the kind attendant had allowed him to use her phone to call both Margaret's cell and home number but he only got voice mail with each of them.

When he'd left that afternoon for the airport, the sun had been shining. But by the time he parked his car at the airport, the snow had started. And when he returned to his car, he had to clear six inches of wet, heavy snow from it.

He forced aside awful scenarios as to what may have happened to Margaret and decided to concentrate on the road. He would try calling her again when he got home.

The road conditions worsened as he left the metropolis of Moncton behind and began his way down the Coverdale Road. And the darkness didn't help the visibility. He was not used to driving in the dark, let alone bad weather

Thankfully the slushy roads were nearly deserted. With it being Christmas Eve, most people were likely at home. Where he should be.

As he headed down into the hills of Albert County, the thick flakes morphed into a smaller, denser form, driven now at an angle by the strengthening wind. His four-wheel-drive had no trouble negotiating the snow and slush, but with the scarcity of roadside lamps, and the white expanse in front of him, he nearly missed the turn-off for the Curryville Road.

There were now no tracks to guide him, and Fred kept his pace slow.

In the six years since his wife Clara had passed, his children continually harangued him to sell the homestead and move into the city, as a lot of his neighbours had done.

But living here kept him healthy, he argued. In the winter he had to continually split wood for the stove which he used for both cooking and heating. That and shovelling the long driveway was more than enough exercise. In the summer months, mowing the large lawn and tending to his garden kept him away from sofa and television.

If he didn't do these things, he knew he would begin the inevitable slide toward a slow death. He was only seventy-one, for Chrissakes. What time he had left, he wanted to spend it here, not cared for by strangers.

"At least get a cell phone," his daughter had pleaded. His argument against this had been that he was never far from home, especially at night and never in bad weather.

Yet, here he was. Maybe he should get one of those damn things and just leave it in the car for instances such as this.

The road sloped down into a hollow that he knew was followed by a steep hill, so he let the vehicle gain a bit of momentum. As he entered the upward grade, he applied more pressure to the gas pedal.

In the middle of the curve at the top of the hill, a shadow flashed into his headlights. He braked hard and the wheels skidded.

Thump!

His fishtailing rear bummer had struck something substantial. He finally got the vehicle to a stop and fumbled in his haste to open his door. As soon as he got it open, a gust of wind wrenched it from his grasp.

He climbed out and immediately gathered the lapels of his unzipped jacket against the bite of the wind. He used his other hand to shield his face from the stinging snow pellets.

"Hello?" Fred shouted.

The only greeting he got was the howl of the wind.

He pushed through the snow to the rear of his car and looked about in the few feet of visibility afforded by his rear lights. He had come very close to sliding into the ditch. Above his head the bare branches of the trees rattled a scolding.

"Hello?" he repeated.

Again, nothing. Maybe it had been a deer that had escaped with a bruising.

By the time he made it back to his still open door, he

was breathless. In that short space of time, the wind had decorated his seat with an inch of snow. He brushed it off and was about to turn to sit down when something tapped on his shoulder.

He whirled about, certain his heart was in irreversible fibrillation.

A stooped man stood in front of him, looking so frail that Fred wondered how he could remain upright against the wind. Wisps of long white hair danced across the nearly bald pate.

"Did – did I hit you?" Fred yelled against the wind.

"No, no! Of course not!"

Fred expelled a gust of air in relief.

"Your back bumper did though."

Fred inhaled and nearly choked on the cold air.

"Just knocked me over into a drift, it did." Although the voice was low and gravelly, his words managed to rise about the wind's howl. "I'm fine! Don't you worry about me!"

Fred opened his back door for the man and waved. "Get in!"

Once they were both inside and the wind had been quieted somewhat, the old man gushed. "Ooh, nice wheels."

Fred twisted in his seat. "You live around here?"

The man grinned so widely his upper denture slipped. "I don't know." He said this as if he was absolutely pleased with himself.

Great, Fred thought. Tonight of all nights he had to bump into a lunatic. "Where do you live?"

That same happy grin followed by another, "I don't know."

Fred swung back around and looked into the storm. What the hell could he do? The closest house was his own. He started the engine.

"I'm going to take you to my place. I'll call around and see if we can get you back home." And out of my hair, Fred didn't add.

"Home?" the old man asked.

"Yeah." Fred looked hopefully into the rear view mirror. "You remember where that is?"

The old man frowned. "I don't think I have one."

Great. Fred sighed and coaxed the car into motion. As he navigated the steep turn into his driveway, he knew immediately something was wrong. He was certain he had turned his porch light on before he had headed into Moncton. But only darkness greeted them.

He left the car lights on to light his way up the steps into the house. Once inside, he discovered neither the phone nor the lights worked. Could things possibly get worse? He had no way of finding out if Margaret was okay plus he was stuck with a bum with no memory.

He located the oil lamp he kept in the porch, and with its feeble light, returned to the car and led the old man into the house.

The old fellow tottered up to the table, his tattered coat and battered shoes dripping snow onto the linoleum. He sat down and grinned at Fred. "Nice place you got here!"

"Yeah," Fred answered glumly as he shoved more wood into the stove.

With crackling enthusiasm, the dry hardwood ignited and soon a soothing warmth chased away the chill.

"You hungry?" Fred asked for lack of anything else to say.

The old man nodded and grinned. "Always!"

Fred brewed some tea and pulled out the plate of Christmas cookies he had bought at Sobey's for Margaret's visit. His visitor gobbled down two immediately, then slurped at his tea.

Fred sighed in exasperation. He checked the phone again. Still dead.

He poured more tea into the fellow's mug. "You sure you don't remember your name or where you live?"

The man sported another sloppy grin. "No, do you?"

"No, well, I know mine of course."

"What is it?"

"Fred."

"Hi, Fred, I'm Hector."

Fred started. "Hector? You just said you didn't know your name."

"I don't but that is what the folks at the Salvation Army call me."

"The Salvation Army?"

"They give out a free Christmas dinner every year. It's delicious."

"Where?"

"I don't know."

How could someone who knew so little be so damned cheerful? Fred sighed and buried his face in his hands. It was going to be a long night. He looked up to see the old man shuffling uninvited into the living room. Fred followed with the lamp.

"Nice tree," said Hector.

Fred stared at the rather pathetic pine he had perched in the corner. Since his wife's death, he had never put up a Christmas tree, decorated, or bought Christmas treats, not even a turkey.

Until this year.

Margaret had outright told him she wanted a tree to decorate when she arrived and she wanted to cook a turkey too. But he settled on the small pitiful thing in front of him and bought a chicken, neither of which would probably get any attention after all. Another stab of worry about Margaret went through him. He checked the phone again. Still dead.

"Where's your family?" Hector asked.

"I'm a widower," Fred forced the words out.

"You have any kids?"

"Yes. Two. And five grandchildren."

The old man looked around, then spread his arms. "Where is everybody?"

Fred sighed. The last thing he felt like doing was chatting with a nut. He would rather go to bed and listen to the wind whose tune, no matter how mournful, always managed to lull him to sleep. He decided to answer this one last question, then go to bed.

"I usually spend Christmas with my son in Saint John, but he and his family are spending Christmas in Texas with my daughter. My sister was supposed to arrive tonight." Fred cut off his words, wondering why he felt he had to explain his being alone on Christmas Eve.

"Ah!" The old man appeared satisfied.

Fred headed for the stairs, then turned to see Hector shuffle over to the piano.

Fred yelled, "Don't touch that!" so sharply, the old man jumped.

That was Clara's piano. Every Christmas Eve she had been alive had been spent gathered around the piano as Clara played. Since her death he had allowed no one to touch it, not even the children. Certainly not this homeless man.

"Just sit there while I get you a blanket and pillow for the couch." He lit another lantern and headed up the narrow stairwell.

When Fred returned he found Hector leafing through one of the albums he had left on the coffee table. He had set them there with the intent of going through them with Margaret while they sipped eggnog and recalled old memories. What else would one do with a sibling they hadn't seen in fifteen years?

Hector appeared to be studying each picture in turn. Fred wanted to yank the album out of the man's hands and tell him to get out of his house.

But he couldn't do that – it was still storming outside.

Hector tapped the photos with a bony finger. "Nice memories. But you need new ones."

But Fred didn't want new memories. He wanted the old ones to not be in the past. Fatigue seeped into Fred's bones. He put the pillow and blanket on the couch beside Hector, and without a word, went up the stairs.

"Merry Christmas, Fred!" the old man yelled after him with all the cheer Fred did not feel.

Fred's bedroom with the soft lamplight and the wind crooning its song, should have felt cozy. But it did not. He lay down fully clothed on the bed and turned down the wick so that only a sliver of light remained, just in case the need for a trip to the bathroom arose. He closed his eyes and tried not to think of the cold empty space beside him. Not for the first time, he wished it had been he who had gone first.

For the first time in years, he dreamt of his wife. It was Christmas Eve, the children were in bed, and she was playing carols for him. The melody to "O Little Town of Bethlehem" tinkled into the stillness of the night.

Fred rolled over. The music sounded so nice. So real.

He jerked upright. The music continued, only now with "Silent Night." The night should damn well be silent, he thought, and struggled out of bed.

He paused at the head of the stairs. It sounded so much like Clara . . . could it be?

He stole down the stairs like a child hoping to see Santa. But it was just the old man. In the flickering lamp light, his face was in shadow, but Fred could see the thin fingers gracefully caressing the keys.

Fred slowly backed up the stairs then sat down upon the top step. If he just listened, it sounded so much like Clara. He could pretend, couldn't he, just for now, that it was her? He pictured her: young, vibrant, and more beautiful than any angel.

***

Fred woke up to a brilliant sun stealing through the small window. Quickly alert in the crisp air of the now cooled house, he leaned over and extinguished the lamp. He listed. All was quiet. No wind. No piano. No movement from downstairs. He couldn't remember returning to bed. Had he dreamt Hector had played the piano?

Downstairs, the lights were on in the living room. He picked up the phone to dial Margaret, but then noticed the blanket and pillow sitting on the couch just as he had placed them the night before. He put down the phone.

"Hector?"

No answer.

The phone pealed out just then, and for the second time in less than a day, Fred feared his heart had lost its rhythm.

"Hello?"

"Fred?" It was Margaret.

"Where are you?"

"In the hospital! I've been trying to reach you all night!"

"We had a storm and the lines have been down. Are you all right?"

"I will be. On my way into the airport last night, I

slipped on some ice, cracked my noggin, and broke my ankle. I'm to have me ankle pinned tomorrow. Oh Fred, I'm so sorry I screwed up Christmas."

"Don't fret about it."

"Ooh, me doctor's here, can I call you later?"

"Sure."

"Merry Christmas!" he heard her say as he hung up.

Well, at least Margaret was okay. Now where had Hector gotten to?"

Fred dressed up in his warmest clothes and stepped outside into a pristine wonderland so bright he had to squint.There were no footprints to indicate Hector had left the house. Unless he had left it hours ago when it was still snowing.

Fred blew out air in frustration as he pondered his options. He could drive into Moncton to the Salvation army and at least let them know Hector was missing.

Yeah, he decided as he headed to his car. A call to the police would be better coming from them, as they knew Hector, and could probably vouch for the senility of the man. Hopefully he'd found another place to shelter.

Drat it! Fred swore to himself. The fellow had no right to make him worry.

Just as grumpy as he'd been on the trip home the night before, Fred drove towards Moncton, going slowly again, only this time so he could look for a tattered grey coat.

The storm had created a beautiful countryside. Snow decorated each and every branch of every bush and tree, telephone line, and pole. The sun's rays glistened off the drifts, and Fred reached for his prescription sunglasses.

In spite of the winter splendour, his grumpiness remained. It was Christmas day, and he should be allowed to wallow at home alone, if that's what he felt like doing. Not chasing after some bum.

The Salvation Army building resembled a beehive, with people scurrying in and out, laden with food containers and supplies. Already a line-up had formed outside although a large sign indicated the kitchen wouldn't be open for another hour.

Inside, Fred found a virtual madhouse. Everyone wore red and green and a headpiece of some sort, either a Santa hat, a green felt hat with pointed ears, or reindeer antlers. If not for the adult-size of those running about, one would think he had stepped into Santa's workshop.

A large woman in a Salvation army uniform barked orders to those around her, and Fred headed towards her.

"Excuse me," he said.

She pointed to a side door. "They need help carving in the kitchen."

"I'm not a volunteer, I'm looking for someone named Hector."

She shook her head, side-mouthed instructions to one of the men, then turned back to Fred. "What area is he helping in?"

"He told me he comes here to eat."

She frowned, then turned to a petite woman tapping her on the arm. Before speaking, she cast a shy smile at Fred. "Leslie, the pies haven't arrived. The baker called to say his truck won't start."

Leslie turned to Fred, "Do you have a vehicle?"

Fred nodded, and only managed to get the word "but" out before the smaller woman was shoved into him.

"Take him," Leslie barked. "And hurry. By the time you get back here, we'll hardly have enough time to slice them up."

Fred opened his mouth to tell this bossy female he didn't take orders from anyone, but the smaller woman looked at him as if her were a hero about to save her from disaster. He swallowed his words, and motioned for her to lead the way.

When he reached his car, he opened the passenger door for her, and helped her up onto the high seat of his SUV. Her warm grateful smile took some of the edge off of his grumpiness.

When he stopped at a light, she held a hand to him. "I'm Barb by the way."

Her grip was gentle, her hand soft. Her lined face was framed in a thick wavy bob.

"Fred."

Although he knew he still sounded gruff and grumpy, she surprised him by giggling.

"You know, I usually don't get into a car with a strange man."

"Well, I usually don't allow strange women to order me around." In fact, there had only been one woman whom he had ever tolerated telling him what to do.

"Oh, Leslie can be bossy, but things sure get done when she's in charge. It's so nice of you to help out on Christmas day. Your family doesn't mind?"

Fred cleared his throat. "My family's all away." He was about to explain that he hadn't come to help out but Barb spoke ahead of him.

"I've been coming since my husband died fifteen years ago. I visit my children and grand-children over Thanksgiving weekend. They're constantly inviting me to spend Christmas with them, but I think they should have their own Christmas, like my husband and I did when our children were young."

Fred agreed with this. His wife had often wanted to invite others to stay at Christmas, but he had always wanted it to be just them and their children.

Then he remembered how, after Clara died, his daughter-in-law had insisted he spend Christmas with them and for the first time he realized how unselfish and generous her offers had been.

"Such wonderful memories," Barb added.

Fred quickly glanced at her, fearful she could read his mind, but she was looking ahead, not focusing, and he knew she was pondering her own memories. Old memories, like he.

"You need new ones," Hector had said.

He was about to ask Barb about Hector, but they had arrived at the bakery.

Two men quickly filled the back of his jeep with pie boxes.

Remembering Leslie's order to return quickly, Fred headed right back to the Salvation Army where Leslie promptly sent them off on new duties. Fred decided he really didn't have anything better to do, so he did as he was told.

He asked everyone he came across about Hector. But no one seemed to know who he was talking about. He figured he would probably have to call the police once he got home.

His resentment of Leslie's bossiness faded with the genuine looks of gratitude and appreciation afforded him by both clients and volunteers. Barb's smile and twinkling blue eyes made him feel especially useful. And he hadn't felt that in a long time.

Perhaps it was the music echoing throughout the hall. Maybe it was the din of cheer mixing with the clatter of dishes. More than once he thought how Clara would have loved to be part of something like this.

Yes, Clara had always been the giver in the family. And he more of a taker, he admitted. Most of the time anyway. He paused and looked about the busy room, grateful for the chance to help out.

When all the patrons had left, the tables cleared and stacked, and the pots and pans washed and stored away,

Fred looked for Barb. To his disappointment, she too seemed to have disappeared.

Surprised at how disappointed he felt, he returned to his Jeep. As he rounded the first corner, he spotted Barb standing at a bus stop. He stopped and leaned over to open the passenger door.

"Need a lift?"

She smiled shyly and shook her head. "No, I'm fine, thanks."

"You can't label me a stranger anymore."

She laughed, then after a pause, climbed in.

Within minutes they reached her apartment building. "Would you like to come in?" she asked. "I could fix us some supper, although I must warn you. I have no turkey, no tree, and no decorations."

Fred thought for a moment. Strangely, he did not want to be alone. Then a thought hit him. This was another opportunity for him to give.

"Well, I have a tree that needs trimming. I've got eggnog, and a chicken we could cook. I even have some Christmas cookies. But I have to warn you, I live in the country. It's a beautiful drive with all the snow we've had," he added.

When she hesitated, he added. "I promise to bring you home safe and sound. I'll give you my phone number, car plate number, my house address, my SI number, my birthdate."

Her laughter stopped him. She pulled a cell phone out of her purse. "I don't need all that, just your phone number and your last name so I can let my daughter know where I am."

Fred watched in wonder as she put his information into her phone, then texted, not called, her daughter. When she put it away, she said with a smile, "And I wouldn't have asked you in if I didn't think you were a good person."

He felt himself blushing and directed the conversation away from himself. "I don't even own a cell phone, nor a computer."

"Well, then I can help you with that," she said. "Until I retired I worked in IT for the phone company. I'm rather a nerd," she added with a bashful smile.

"Well, I could use a nerd now and then," Fred said as he put the car into gear.

They were soon out of the city and in the hills of Albert County. "What a beautiful drive. I'm glad you asked me."

"Me too," echoed Fred.

"New memories," she said.

Fred started. "What did you say?"

"New memories. We can keep our old ones, but we should try to make new ones too. I'm so glad you decided to help out this year."

"I have to admit, I didn't really come to help. I was looking for someone named Hector. He said he ate there every year."

Her eyes widened with recognition. "Hector?"

"Yes, do you know him?"

"Well, we used to have a Hector that came from the nursing home up the street. He suffered from dementia. Every Christmas he would escape from the home and find his way to the Salvation Army for Christmas dinner. After a while, the nursing home arranged his trip there and back. But Fred, why would you be looking for him? He passed away nearly five years ago."

Fred tried to shrug off the chill that tickled his back. "It must have been someone else then. An old man named Hector spent the night at my place. The phone lines were down and I couldn't call anyone. This morning he was gone." He hesitated, not sure he wanted to know the answer to his next question. "What did your Hector look like?"

"Thin, always wore a gray overcoat. The nurses said he slept in it. He had long wispy white hair, but was bald on top. Although forgetful, he was always so cheerful . . . Fred, are you okay? You've gone pale."

Fred glanced over at her. "You still want to have dinner with someone who sees ghosts?"

Barb smiled. "Christmas is the time for ghosts." After a moment, she added, "And memories."

"Yes," Fred said. "Both old and new."

GHOST OF A CHANCE

Dan Edison glanced at his watch. Oh Lord, where were they? Their plane had landed over a half-hour ago. Ample time for them to find their way to the baggage area. Had his daughter changed her mind?

He glanced through the teeming crowd of weary adults, sullen teenagers, and crying children. No Lauren. To escape the chaos, he turned toward the glass doors, but the congestion of limos, buses, and taxis provided no relief.

Dan knew the real reason for his anxiety was the special baggage accompanying his daughter. And he could blame no one but himself for opening *that* door.

When Lauren had called on the anniversary of her mother's death, their conversation had begun like all the others, brief, polite chats void of any real communication.

When he sensed she was about to hang up, he asked about her job at a private school north of Houston.

She hesitated, no doubt surprised by his chattiness. Her response, a shaky 'okay', hinted that all was not okay. A glimmer of hope that perhaps she and Sam were breaking up sliced through him.

"What's wrong, Lauren?"

"Nothing, really. Things have been a little hectic. Sam's latest promotion has her traveling to Europe a lot."

Dan bit down on the "Really?" that wanted to jump out of his mouth, but he knew she would hear the optimism in his voice.

Lauren went on. "This wouldn't normally be a problem, but Maria, our nanny, was seriously injured in a car accident last week."

"Will she be all right?"

"She suffered a crushed pelvis but, thank God, she's on the mend. The only thing is, she won't be able to look after Bobby until after Christmas."

Bobby. Dan bit down on more words straining to get out. Words that would insist that the product of Sam's egg and some anonymous donor's sperm was Sam's problem, not Lauren's.

Dan forced himself to stay positive. "You'll find someone."

"We're interviewing now, but it'll be hard to find a temporary replacement, especially at this time of year."

We. The word snuffed out Dan's remaining whiff of optimism. He couldn't fathom the 'we'. If Lauren asked him to walk on the moon, he would try his darnedest to get there. But this 'we' shit. An alternative response came to him. "Can't one of you take time off from work?"

"Sam certainly can't. We did manage to find a day-home that'll take Bobby during school hours."

"Well, that doesn't sound so bad," he offered.

"Oh, it's okay for now. But . . ."

Dan waited silently for the conversation to continue. For the first time in several years, he and Lauren were actually talking.

Her sigh sounded full of reluctance. "I've been asked to display some of my paintings in Boston next week. I'll be gone five days and Sam will be in Europe. That's the problem. We have no one to look after Bobby full time."

The fact that Lauren had revealed this much touched Dan and he genuinely wanted to help. But what could he do?

After an awkward silence, Lauren said, "Didn't mean to dump on you, Dad. Talk to you at Christmas."

The dial tone droned in Dan's ear. This conversation, though longer, had ended like all the others. With no real goodbye. Before he could think about it, he punched in Lauren's number.

To his horror another woman answered. Sam. Since the day Lauren first brought Samantha home, Dan had not spoken a word to the woman who had destroyed his and his wife's hope of having grandchildren.

He cleared his throat, but before he could choke out any words, the woman said, "Hold on, Mr. Edison. I'll get Lauren," in a smooth tone surprisingly void of resentment.

"Hello?" Lauren asked.

Oh Lord. What could he do? Offer to go to Houston? No. In his last face-to-face conversation with Lauren on the day of Winnie's funeral, he'd said some horrible things about Sam. Granted, he'd been grief-stricken, but still . . .

"Dad?"

"Um . . . is Bobby still in diapers?" No way could he handle diapers. He'd never been able to stomach the foul messes his daughter had produced. Boys were surely worse.

"Dad, he's four."

The words were slightly garbled, as if Lauren were trying not to giggle. Surely that meant the kid was housebroken. How hard could it be? Five days. One hundred and twenty hours.

"Dad?" Lauren interrupted before Dan could compute the minutes.

"Uh, could he stay here with me?" His words came out in a rushed breath.

The silence that followed gave him far too much time to regret his offer.

"Are you sure? Maybe you should think about this first."

"No, no." He knew he'd retract the offer if he did that.

"Let me run this by Sam and I'll call you back."

Dan had three short minutes to harbor a slim hope that Sam would not agree to the proposal. But Lauren called back full of excitement.

New worries filled Dan's head. "Uh, what do I feed him?"

Her soft laugh reminded Dan so much of Winnie his chest tightened. "He's not a dog or a cat. He has a full set of teeth and no allergies. Just keep the sweet stuff to a minimum, as it makes him a little hyper."

Hyper? Oh Lord. "Well, then. How do we get him here?"

"I'll fly with him to Halifax, spend a couple of hours with the two of you, then fly back to Boston."

Three short weeks and a lot of regret later, here he stood in the baggage area, his dread building every second.

"Daddy?"

The familiar child-like question startled him. He swung around, half expecting to see ten-year-old Lauren eager to show her daddy something neat. Instead an adult stood in front of him. Lauren's thirty years had given her a maturity that only enhanced her beauty. Her right hand rested proudly on the head of a child who appeared much too tall for a four-year-old.

"He's – he's so big." Dan wondered how a former journalist and so-called writer could articulate so poorly.

Bright blue eyes, enlarged with what could be fear, blinked up at him. "No, YOU'RE big!"

Lauren's attempt at a smile revealed her own awkwardness. "He's tall for his age. Bobby, say hello to your grandfather."

Dan tried not to grimace at the address. This lad shared no gene pool with him.

"Is he a giant, Mommy Lauren?"

Mommy Lauren? Oh, Lord.

Lauren fidgeted with her purse. "No. He's just tall." She finally looked up, her eyes full of apology. "I'm sorry. I thought we'd have a couple of hours to, you know, chat but we got delayed in Houston and my plane to Boston is already boarding."

Dan's urge to comfort his daughter diminished his own tension. He put a hand on the boy's shoulder. "We'll be fine. Give me the claim checks for his luggage."

She pulled a wrinkled airline folder out of her coat pocket. Dan could picture Lauren sitting on the plane, her hand in her pocket, crumpling the contents in anxiety.

"There's just one bag. He'll need a warmer jacket and boots. I didn't have time to buy them before we left. Would you mind buying some for him and I'll pay you when I get back?"

"Er, sure. No problem." Big problem, he thought.

She knelt down and hugged Bobby. "I'll miss you." The smile she gave her child was forced. "Be good for Grampa, will you?"

Grampa? Oh, Lord.

Bobby nodded.

Lauren stood up. "Thanks, Dad. I really appreciate this."

After a glance at her watch and a hesitant hug, she

scurried to the security check in. She turned around at the corner, waved once, then disappeared, but not before Dan caught the glimmer of tears in her eyes. His throat tightened with an unexpected wave of emotion. He wanted to run after his daughter. Hold her. Tell her everything would be all right.

She had always been 'Daddy's girl'. Even after she left for university, they remained close and talked often. But all ties were severed the moment Lauren brought Sam home. Winnie had constantly tried to mend things between them, even suggesting they go to Houston for Bobby's first Christmas. When Dan refused, Winnie went without him. In the ensuing years she would often remind Dan, "Until you accept Sam, you don't stand a ghost of a chance of having a relationship with your daughter."

Dan stared at the corner Lauren had disappeared around. Winnie's words still rang true. Dan felt a tug on his sleeve. He looked down at his responsibility for the next five days and wondered what the hell he had gotten himself into.

"Okay, let's find your bag." He hoped he sounded less frightened than he felt. "Do you know what it looks like?"

Bobby nodded solemnly. "Black."

Dan barely managed to wedge the two of them into the mob double-parked at the turnstile. He looked at the luggage passing by. Nearly every bag was black.

"Is it big or small?"

Bobby shrugged. "Sorta big."

Oh Lord.

After several minutes, Bobby pointed to a black duffel bag. "That one."

Dan grabbed it. As they turned to leave, a young man said, "Excuse me, I believe that's mine."

Dan examined the ticket. Sure enough, he had grabbed

the wrong bag. Swallowing his embarrassment, he grunted, "Sorry." Three duffel bags later, he found one whose tag matched the ticket.

"Stay close now," Dan said. To ensure the lad didn't run off, he took hold of Bobby's jacket collar.

Bobby twisted free and coughed. "I need to breathe, you know."

Sassy, thought Dan, but said nothing as Bobby reached up and placed a small warm hand in his.

"There, isn't that better?" Bobby asked in a tone that bordered on condescending.

Sassy.

As Dan buckled Bobby into the back seat, the lad said, "I don't think I like Canda."

"Canada."

"Canda's too cold."

Dan expected continued whining on the way home, but before he had pulled onto the highway, a glance in the rearview mirror revealed Bobby's sleeping form slumped against the shoulder strap. This allowed Dan to concentrate on navigating the dark, narrow roads, which, thanks to the current provincial government's lack of fiscal skills, were more pitted than the surface of the moon. He succeeded in dodging all but two of the potholes. So much for his recent front-end alignment.

The moment Dan pulled into the driveway, Bobby sat up and rubbed his eyes. Once inside the front door, the boy said, "It's cold in here. Almost as cold as outside."

Dan pulled off his boots. "I'll light the stove for us."

The efficient wood stove on the lower level heated the four-level-split more economically than electricity. Each spring, Dan ordered in eight-foot lengths of hardwood, then cut and split them himself. Not bad for a man nearing sixty-two, he figured. He proceeded to untie Bobby's shoes.

Bobby backed away. "I wear my shoes in the house at home."

"Well, here we take them off. If your feet get cold, I'll buy you a pair of slippers."

Bobby wrinkled his nose in puzzlement and Dan was smacked with a memory of Lauren doing that same thing as a child.

Bobby watched quietly as Dan stacked the stove. The dry kindling quickly caught. When the larger logs began to flame, Dan shut the doors and partially closed the flue. "There, it'll be warm in no time."

"We don't have one of those at home," Bobby offered.

"I'll bet."

"I need to pee."

Oh, Lord. "Do you need help?"

His blue eyes impossibly larger than before, Bobby looked at Dan like he was crazy. "I was toilet trained just after I turned two."

"Oh." Dan led him to the bathroom across the hall. "You remember that?"

"No, but that's what Mom says to the other moms at day care."

Mom. Bobby's name for Sam, no doubt. And Lauren was 'Mommy Lauren'. Dan turned on the light switch then just managed to yank his hand clear before Bobby slammed the door shut. Dan breathed a sigh of relief when it sounded like the stream was hitting the target.

Given the late hour, Dan took Bobby directly up to the third level to Lauren's old room. The multicolored quilt that Winnie had crafted for Lauren's seventh birthday lay upon the bed. The same quilt beneath which Winnie had spent her last night. During bouts of insomnia, Winnie would often retreat to Lauren's room so she wouldn't disturb Dan's sleep. Her thoughtfulness haunted him still.

"Want to get into your pajamas?" Dan asked.

Bobby vigorously shook his head as he climbed onto the bed. "No. Canda's too cold."

"Canada," Dan corrected. "Here, crawl inside the quilts. There, like that." Dan tucked the blankets up around the child's chin. "You'll be toasty in a second."

"I don't like toast."

There was a lot this kid didn't like. "Want me to leave the lamp on?"

As Bobby nodded, his bottom lip quivered. "When's Mommy Lauren coming back?"

Not soon enough, Dan thought. "She'll be back in a few days. We'll have some fun tomorrow."

Doubt registered on the round face.

Dan pushed aside his own uncertainty. "We'll go to the mall and buy you some warm clothes." That ought to kill a few hours. "Now try to sleep."

Dan went into his office next door and shut his computer off. He was in no mood for writing. Since leaving the newspaper seven years before, he still submitted articles for the weekend edition. It helped pass the time. Particularly in winter with the golf course closed.

When he looked back into the guest room, he was relieved to see the boy's eyes shut.

This might not be so bad, he thought.

* * *

Dan patted the warm lump beside him and grinned. Winnie would be pissed if she caught Fanny in their bed.

But the cool air quickly cleared his head. Winnie was gone. Fanny too. Then what the hell? He started to turn over when up popped a head topped with spiked brown hair. Startled, Dan lurched backward and, in spite of desperate flailing, slid rather unceremoniously onto the floor.

Bobby leaned over the bed and erupted into giggles. Dan bristled and was about to deliver a stern lecture as to what should or should not be considered funny when the small lad sobered and asked, "You okay?" in a tone so sincere it melted Dan's anger.

"What are you doing in here?" he asked.

"I was cold. I miss Sprout."

"Sprout?"

"My kitten. He sleeps with me and keeps me warm."

"Houston's hot. Why do you need a kitten to keep you warm?"

"Cause of the air condishner. Mommy Lauren likes to have it cold when she sleeps."

Mommy Lauren. Would he ever get used to this? Dan rolled over onto his knees.

"Besides, the lady said I could sleep with you."

Dan felt a chill that did not originate from kneeling on a cold hardwood floor. "Lady? What lady?"

"The lady in my room."

The air suddenly seemed scarce. Dan attempted a few breaths before he ventured to speak. "Wha-what did she look like?"

Bobby shrugged. "A lady."

Though he had always accompanied Winnie to church, Dan had not shared her belief in the afterlife. When someone died, that was the end. Wasn't it? Surely, if Winnie haunted this house, he would have seen her before now. Using the bed for leverage, Dan pushed upright and concentrated on reality. "Let's get some breakfast. You don't like toast, right?"

"Nope."

"How about oatmeal?"

Bobby wrinkled his nose.

O Lord.

∗ ∗ ∗

"Now stay close." In spite of it being a weekday, shoppers filled the mall. Dan had wanted to arrive early to avoid the crowds but it had taken awhile to get Bobby fed, bathroomed, and out the door. Dan scanned the shops as they walked, looking for a store that sold children's clothing, hoping he didn't run into someone he knew. Bobby would be too hard to explain.

The lad mumbled something about Christmas, but Dan couldn't hear him above the din. He noticed the large, seasonally-lit Sears sign a short distance away. "Let's try in there."

When Bobby didn't answer, Dan looked down. The lad was gone. Dan swung around, darting his gaze behind and in front of every person in the near vicinity.

"Bobby? Bobby!"

A nearby woman frowned at him accusingly.

Dan hurriedly retraced his steps, calling for the boy. He forced himself into the role of a quarterback rather than the preferred linebacker as he negotiated the populated hallway. Panic rendered his search ineffective and he tried to calm down, but thoughts of trying to explain to Lauren how he had lost Bobby kept him moving in circles, glancing everywhere and focusing on nothing.

He forced himself to a halt in the center of the mall where a crowd had gathered to listen to a choir. A plan jumbled into place. He would interrupt the music and make an announcement. Surely, someone had seen Bobby.

As he pushed his way toward the singers, the organ-accompanied rendition of "Little Drummer Boy" grew louder.

"Excuse me," he began, hardly recognizing the squeaky voice as his own. He cleared his throat then repeated his words. Like a bad dream, no one seemed to hear him. He was ready to scream when he felt a tug on his arm.

There stood Bobby smiling up at him. Saying something. By the time Dan dragged the boy out into an open area, anger had eroded Dan's worry.

"Where the hell did you go? Didn't I tell you to stay close?"

Instead of answering, Bobby covered his ears.

Dan yanked the small hands down. "Now you listen to me."

"Your voice is so loud I can still listen with my ears covered."

During her childhood, Lauren had done that very same thing on more than one occasion. Winnie had often cautioned Dan to lower his deep voice for the sake of all the neighbors. He knelt down on one knee in front of Bobby. Fighting for control, he lowered his voice. "Now, look. A mall is a dangerous place. A stranger could have taken you!"

A pout accentuated the already thick lips. "But I heard the same songs in church and Mommy Lauren says that church is a safe place."

Church? It would have pleased Winnie to know Lauren was introducing the child to religion.

Bobby's pout faded into a quiver. The large eyes grew wet.

Oh Lord. "Look, Bobby. I was really worried about you."

Bobby wiped his nose with his hand and sniffed. Wishing the kid had sniffed first Dan gave Bobby his hankerchief. Bobby blew into it, then handed it back to Dan. Grasping the cloth between thumb and index, Dan tried to stuff it into his pocket with as little contact as possible. He pointed at the Sears sign.

"Let's go get you a jacket," he said, trying to sound optimistic and calm his hammering heart at the same time. Now would not be the time t have a heart attack.

Two inquiries later, Dan found himself surrounded by racks of ski pants and jackets. From nearby Toyland, a child's petulant wail instilled a sense of urgency. He picked up a jacket. "How's this one?"

"I don't like red."

Oh Lord. "What color do you like?"

"Blue."

Dan chose a navy one.

Bobby nodded.

Hey, this wasn't so bad. As Dan approached the counter, a woman hurried over. She smiled briefly at Dan, then beamed at Bobby. "Hello! Are you out shopping?"

Bobby nodded.

"Is this for your brother?" she asked.

"I don't have one yet. But Mommy Lauren says maybe next year.

For the second time that day, Dan had trouble finding enough air. Exhilaration and fear dueled within him.

The woman's laugh was gentle and strangely soothing. "T'is the season for nice surprises, isn't it? Then who is this jacket for?"

"Me, isn't it, Grampa?"

"Well, er, uh . . ."

Dan looked at the woman, whose warm smile reached her eyes. EUNICE, her nametag read. She was, he guessed, in her late fifties. No doubt a grandparent as well. Something Dan had never thought . . . oh Lord.

"This jacket is too big for your grandson."

"Oh. Uh, how can you tell?"

Another smile. She stepped from behind the counter. "Let me help you pick something out."

Ten minutes later Bobby pranced in a perfectly fitting blue snowsuit and boots. After donning matching mittens and toque, he poised in front of a mirror.

Just as Dan was about to thank the kind woman, whom he now knew to have four grandchildren, Bobby moaned.

Oh, Lord, what now?

Eunice knelt beside the child. "What's wrong, Bobby?"

"First I was cold. Now, I'm too hot!"

Eunice laughed as she unzipped the jacket and pulled it gently off Bobby's shoulders. "Outside, this will be just right. It's too warm in here, that's all."

"It's cold in Grampa's house. Really cold. But that's okay, cause Grampa's better than a kitty in bed!"

Once again Dan was rendered speechless. And to his horror, he felt a flush creep up his cheeks.

But Eunice, bless her soul, chatted on with Bobby about Santa while she rang up the bill.

"Santa's gonna bring me a Turboblaster, especially if I do what Grampa says."

Dan didn't have time to ask what a Turboblaster was before Eunice said, "Oh, those are so much fun! They can shoot water so far! And in Houston, you can play with it all year round. The water would freeze here."

Bobby giggled. "Yeah. Like me."

Eunice must have pushed Bobby's chat button and long before Dan reached home he wished he knew how to shut it off. Answering all the questions made him tired. By the time they reached the house, huge flakes drifted slowly downward from heavy clouds that promised more. He'd have to get the snow blower out the next day, he figured. Then he wondered how he could clear the driveway and watch Bobby at the same time.

Would it be considered child abuse if he used a leash?

* * *

Dan woke when he felt the bed compress under the weight of a small body. The clock informed him it was nearing midnight. Turning over, he said, "Want me to change the hot water bottle for you?"

Bobby shook his head. "The lady said it was okay for me to sleep in here."

It took Dan only a moment to think of an answer. "Well, I guess then it must be okay."

After a few rotations, Bobby became still. Dan waited a few minutes longer. Then as stealthily as was possible for a stiff senior citizen, he slipped from beneath the comforter. Once upright, he paused. Assured the bundle on the bed hadn't moved, Dan navigated through the familiar darkness to the hallway and down to Lauren's old room. The brilliant white of the snow-covered land stole through the window and cast an eerie sheen upon the room's contents.

Dan walked over to the bed, straightened the sheets, and smoothed the quilt, letting his hands linger where Winnie had last lain.

He had read somewhere that children could sense spirits more readily than adults. Had Bobby seen Winnie?

A cool draft caressed his neck and he whipped around looking for its source. An examination of the windowsill detected no cold air penetrating past his recent calking. Dan returned to his original position by the bed but could only sense a dark emptiness. He sighed and turned toward the door. Through the window, he had noticed that while clouds still hid the stars, it had stopped snowing. In the morning he would clear the driveway. Physical activity always relieved this heavy feeling.

When he returned to bed, Bobby stirred. Dan turned his back to the lad, not in the mood for conversation. Without a word, Bobby nestled against Dan's back. To his surprise, Dan found the warm lump soothing. The weight upon his chest lifted and he drifted into a restful sleep.

* * *

The next morning revealed a good six inches of snow on the driveway. After breakfast, Dan helped an eager Bobby into his snowsuit, an effort that left droplets of sweat on Dan's brow. Bobby remained close to Dan's heels as he brought the snow blower out from the shed, but once it was ready to go, Dan perched the lad on the porch.

"Now promise me you won't leave the porch?"

Bobby nodded.

After a few glances to ensure Bobby was still on the porch, Dan relaxed and allowed himself to fall into the peaceful mental zone that accompanies repetitive labor.

As he cleared a second row, his heart stopped when he spotted Bobby waving to him from atop the porch railing. Dan shut the machine off and raced toward the house. "Get down!"

Bobby looked behind him and teetered.

"No! Wait until I get there!"

The moment Dan set Bobby down, the lad covered his ears and shouted. "I didn't leave the porch!"

Dan pulled the boy's hands down and forced himself to speak calmly. "No. But you could have fallen!"

"But I couldn't see over this!" A mitten-clad hand slapped the railing.

"Oh." Dan thought a moment. "Wait here." He fetched a chair from the kitchen. Only as he opened the door to go back out did he notice the puddles of melting snow marking his footsteps. Winnie would have given him shit, he thought. Then he decided, no she wouldn't have. She would have joined Bobby on the porch. And perhaps on the railing as well.

Dan set Bobby onto the chair. "There, you should be able to see now. Don't fall off the chair."

Bobby threw his arms around Dan's neck. "Thanks, Grampa."

The hug felt so warm, so right, Dan found himself responding. "You're welcome. Now be careful!"

Dan resumed his work. The next time he neared the house, he could hear Bobby giggling. Dan found the deep gurgle both rejuvenating and infectious. He did a little dance as he turned the machine around and was rewarded with resounding chortles deep enough to be coming from a large man. He could almost hear Winnie saying to Bobby, "Grampa's a goof!"

When the driveway was clear, Dan paused to inhale the crisp air. He felt good. Damned good.

"Are you finished?" Bobby asked.

"Yep. All done."

"Can you do another one?"

"Another what?"

"Driveway. What about that one over there?" Bobby pointed down the street to where Dan's nearest neighbor, Annie Ferguson, lived.

Dan hesitated. He knew Annie looked forward to her son's visits and, though he only lived 45 minutes away, he didn't come by very often. There was another reason for Dan's hesitation. He would have to explain Bobby, then Sam and Lauren's . . . situation. Just thinking about it was difficult enough, let alone talking about it.

"Uh, that belongs to Mrs. Ferguson. Her son usually comes to do it."

"What if he doesn't?"

"Then . . . maybe. We'll see." Dan groped for a change of subject. "Want to see what's on television?"

As he watched the lad race up the steps, Dan prayed that Bobby would forget all about Annie Ferguson's driveway.

* * *

As soon as Bobby's feet touched the floor the next morning, he raced to a window. His exuberant announcement that 'Mrs. Furson's' driveway had not been cleared initiated a dread Dan could not shake.

"Mrs. Fer-gus-on," Dan corrected.

"Yeah, Mrs. Furson. Mom says I have a good memory. And Mommy Lauren says I'm real smart."

"I'm sure you are," Dan quickly replied. "Your enunciation could use some work."

Bobby wrinkled his nose.

After failing to get the lad to finish his oatmeal, even with double the allotment of brown sugar, Dan let the boy struggle into his snowsuit while he internally debated how he was going to answer the pending questions from Annie.

The raw bite to the wind gave Dan hope that Annie would stay inside while he cleared her driveway. The second he was finished, he would head home right away. Turn it into a race with Bobby. Yeah, this just might work. When they rounded the curve of the street, Bobby let out a groan.

The Ferguson driveway, now stripped of snow, gleamed blackly between white banks. While they were eating breakfast, the son must have come and gone.

Bobby's disappointment was as palpable as Dan's relief.

"My, you're strong," Dan commented as he let Bobby help him push the snow blower back home.

Bobby didn't respond. He kept his head down as if concentrating on putting one shiny boot in front of the other. No whining. No crying. A real little man, Dan thought.

At the mention of renting some movies, Bobby cheered up considerably. They picked out three with a Christmas theme. After starting the first one, *Miracle on 34ᵗʰ Street*, Dan supplied the lad with slices of cheese and an apple before heading up to his computer.

He had a deadline coming up. Each year he wrote a seasonal piece for his column in the weekend section of The Halifax Chronicle. Winnie had always given him ideas. Since her death, the project had become increasingly difficult. Though he had tried to end his recent stories with some semblance of hope, he knew his editor had found the articles a little dark.

"Give me something more humorous this year, Dan," Bob had said. "Something more along the lines of what your readers are used to."

Here it was just a week away from the deadline and Dan hadn't even started. What could he write about? He was no Dickens. *A Christmas Carol* and its Tiny Tim made him think of the young lad downstairs. And the 'lady' Bobby claimed to have seen. Dan had refrained from questioning the child further, unwilling to broach that painful subject.

Since Winnie's death, he had neither openly nor privately shed tears. Real men controlled their emotions, in spite of exhibitions to the contrary by the sissies currently dominating the movie screens.

Bobby. Hmm. He could write about a child's first Christmas in Canada, or, Canda, as Bobby would say. A land of ice and snow where it was colder outside than in. The opposite of Houston and its proverbial air conditioning. Snow suits, kittens, and cold nights. Turboblasters shooting icicles. Dan's fingers flew in response to the images popping into his head. He grinned as the protagonist moaned about his snowsuit being too hot and that he would never be just right. For the first time in years, Dan felt in 'the zone'.

The ringing phone rudely interrupted his train of thought.

"Hello, Dan!" Annie's chirpy voice filled his ear.

It took a lot of effort to respond with a semblance of cheer.

"I have a favor to ask," she said.

Oh Lord.

"Smith's Tree Farm dropped off the Christmas tree I ordered, but I was taking a nap and didn't hear the door bell. They were supposed to bring it in and set it up. Both Joe and Emily's families are coming to spend the weekend. I want to surprise them with the tree and decorations."

She paused for breath, but only for a second. "Two

whole days with everyone here! Can you believe it?"

"That sounds lovely." For Annie. Not Dan. All of Annie's grandchildren were school age and he could imagine the din. No thanks. "Uh, when do you want to put it up?"

"Well, I don't want to inconvenience you. I . . . uh," As soon as possible, she was too polite to add.

Annie was sure to latch onto Bobby and feed him cookies. Old people did that. Then the questions would come. Awkward questions with even more awkward answers.

Dan glanced at his watch. Three-fifteen! Oh Lord. Bobby had been watching television for over three hours. Would the lad be able to sit still for yet another few minutes?

Annie interjected into his hesitation. "It shouldn't take long. I have the stand all set up."

"I'll be right over."

Dan cut off the tirade of gratitude with a brisk "No problem." Annie certainly sounded happy. He knew she usually went to either Joe's house in Truro or Emily's home in Halifax for Christmas, and she was probably getting high on the anticipation of all of them coming here.

Winnie always went nuts at Christmas time, sometimes starting her shopping and preparation plans as early as September. Before the end of November she would decorate every inch of the house and invite everyone she knew for their annual Christmas party.

Of course, that had ended with Winnie's death. Dan disliked crowds and didn't miss all the fuss. Christmas was just another day. With his bridge club members and golf buddies otherwise occupied, he often wrote two or three articles that he could use in good weather months.

He went downstairs to find Bobby still prone in front

of the television. Dan gasped when he saw what was on: a soap opera. And a rather steamy one at that.

"Oh Lord!" He pushed the off button. "What happened to the movie?"

"It finished."

"Well, how about this one?" Dan inserted *Rudolph* into the machine. When Bobby re-entered his trance, Dan went downstairs.

As he pulled on his overshoes, Bobby's head popped over the railing. "Where you going?"

"Just over to Mrs. Ferguson's for a minute. I'll be right back."

Bobby responded as Dan had feared he would. "Can I come?"

"Uh, no. I'll only be gone a few minutes. It's cold out. You'd have to get all dressed up again, and she's in a hurry. She's waiting for me." Dan spat his sentences out quickly, hoping to avoid the much dreaded tantrum.

But after only a brief solemn stare, Bobby disappeared, most likely to return to the television.

An outburst would have made it easier to leave him, Dan thought as he hurriedly donned his coat. He attempted to exhale some of his guilt as he stepped off the porch. He glanced back. Bobby's somber face peered at him through the second floor window.

Dan could almost feel Winnie's disdain. *For once, swallow that damned Edison pride!* Dan knew he could ignore Winnie's words, as he had on more than one occasion during their marriage, but he doubted he could ever erase the image of that sad face in the window.

He turned around and headed back onto the porch. By the time he opened the door, Bobby was struggling to slide into his slippery snow pants.

"You won't need the pants. Your jacket and boots will do."

The shine in the boy's eyes eased some of the dread that had replaced Dan's guilt.

"Oh, look at the tree!" Bobby squealed when they rounded the corner. A plump fir filled half of Annie's driveway.

Annie came from around the side of the house carrying a small sled. The nicks on the runners and the faded red paint indicated it had been well used. She waved at Bobby. "Well hello!" She paused to lean the sled at an angle behind a basket filled with cone-laden pine branches and fresh holly drooping with berries. Strings of lights adorned the hedge. Annie had been busy. After adjusting the angle of the sled, she strolled over with her hand held out to Bobby.

Dan took a breath, then said, "Bobby, this is Mrs. Ferguson."

Annie gave Bobby's mitten a vigorous shake. "I'm so pleased to meet you, Bobby! Thanks for coming to help."

Bobby pointed to the sled. "What's that?"

"This is an antique sled. Many years ago my brothers and I used to slide down the hills on it every winter. It's my little ghost of Christmas Past. It reminds me of all the wonderful years I had growing up."

Eager to get the pending scene over with, Dan lifted the tree up. It was none too light. "Bobby, you help steer from the front."

Bobby scurried ahead grabbed the treetop.

"I'll get the door!" Annie went up the steps with the eagerness of a child going to meet Santa.

Grasping the top tightly, Bobby marched up the steps, his posture as proud as a prince. Just inside the porch door, with Dan at the bottom of the steps and feeling the full weight of the tree, Bobby paused.

"Keep going," Dan barked. He couldn't hold this thing forever.

"My boots!" the lad wailed.

"Oh, d'on't worry about your boots," Annie chirped. "It's been way too long since I've had to clean a bit of snow off the linoleum!"

Dan appreciated this too, as he was breathing heavily by the time he stepped inside the door. He feared if he put the tree down, he might not be able to pick it up again.

Annie had the stand all ready and with her help, the task of uprighting and securing the tree proved easier than Dan had anticipated. The crown nearly reached the ceiling and the thick wide branches filled the entire corner.

Annie clasped her hands in front of her. "Oh, my. It's lovely! They didn't even charge me for delivery." She gave Dan a knowing glance. "They also have an area where people can go and cut down their own tree."

Whenever he and Winnie had socialized with Annie and Bill, Dan had often considered Annie a trifle bossy. But her current suggestion was a good one. Getting a tree would give him and Bobby something to do the next day. Then the following day, the eve of Bobby's departure, could be spent trimming it. The end was in sight.

"Now let me take your coats." Annie already had Bobby's half off.

"Uh . . . we should be going."

"I wouldn't hear of it." Annie planted herself in front of the door. "I've some cookies in the kitchen that need taste testing."

"But . . ." Dan began.

Annie waved him off. "You can spare a few minutes so I can repay two gentlemen for their endeavors."

Bossy, thought Dan. He was about to say no when he felt a tug on his sleeve.

Bobby, already freed of his coat and boots, grinned up

at him. "Take your coat off, Grampa!"

Grampa. Oh Lord.

To his relief, Annie showed no sign she had heard as she led the way to the kitchen.

"Pull up a chair, boys. Dan, coffee or tea?"

Nothing. Just let us go home. "Uh, tea." After a pause, he blurted out, "Please."

"And Bobby, what would you like?"

"Tea," Bobby stated boldly. Then he too added, "please."

"Then tea for all of us," Annie said, sparing Dan the decision as to whether a four-year-old should be allowed to drink tea.

Annie gave them each a plate decorated with holly and a matching paper napkin.

Bobby carefully unfolded his napkin and placed in on his lap with the proficiency of a Lord at the Queen's table. Dan felt a surge of pride, though his continuing dread tainted it.

Annie placed a tray laden with several kinds of sweets in the center of the table. "You can have one while you wait for your tea," she whispered loudly in Bobby's ear. She smiled at Dan and said, "Grampa can have one too."

Grampa. For lack of anything else to do, Dan chose a date square because it looked just like the ones Winnie used to make. And it tasted like it too. Too much so. A wave of emotion washed over him. What the hell was the matter with him?

Annie placed three mugs onto the table. Bobby's mocha-colored brew contrasted with the black tea in the others.

In response to Bobby's comparing eyes, Annie said, "I figured you'd like yours better with lots of milk and honey. And a wee bit of chocolate. Try it."

"Mmmm," Bobby responded.

The silence that accompanied their ingestion of sweets compounded Dan's agitation. It didn't help when he noticed Annie watching him. Instinctively he knew she was about to pounce. Oh Lord. The neighbors would have lots to talk about this holiday season.

Annie turned to Bobby. "Do you have a quilt with horses and dogs and cats on it?"

Bobby's eyes widened. He nodded. "Mommy Lauren says Grandma made me that quilt."

"And I helped her make it. She was so excited about her new grandson."

Dan's air escaped in a rush. Of course. Winnie and Annie had attended the same quilting guild. And bridge club. No doubt his forthright wife had told Annie about Lauren. And Sam. And Bobby. How could he not have realized this? Then he recalled how he had stubbornly refused to allow Winnie to broach the topic. There was no way he could have known who she told and who she didn't.

"How is Lauren, Dan?" Annie's direct look hinted that she wanted an equally direct answer.

Dan cleared his throat. "Uh . . . she's in Boston. She has an exhibit there of her paintings."

"How exciting! I didn't know she painted. She still teaching?"

Bobby answered first. "She teaches grade three at the school I'll be going to next year. May I have another cookie, please?"

"Of course. Goodness, what a polite young man Lauren and Samantha are raising. You must be really proud, Dan."

Dan looked over at Bobby. "Yes, I am," he said, and realized his heavy dread had dissipated and been replaced by an unfamiliar calm. Only then did he notice the decorations and ornaments adorning every available space on mantle, walls, and furniture. The fragrance of the fresh cut fir wafted from the nearby living room and mingled with the spicy aroma of baking. Seasonal tunes tingled from the old stereo in the corner. It all seemed so right. Almost magical.

Dan said, "The place looks great, Annie. Your family will be thrilled."

Annie's eyes gleamed. "They wanted me to go with them to Hawaii for Christmas, but I can't make that long trip. So they decided to come here and celebrate with me before they go. What fun I've had with the baking and decorating! We'll have a tree trimming party on Friday. You and Bobby should drop in."

"Thanks, but Bobby's flying back to Houston that day."

Annie accompanied them out onto the step. Before following Bobby down the driveway, Dan turned back. "Uh, thanks, Annie. For today." He hesitated, then added, "And for being Winnie's friend."

Annie's eyes misted over. "I still miss her. As I'm sure you do. Winnie would be so happy to know you and Lauren have reconciled."

Dan's chest tightened. Something must have showed on his face, as Annie went on.

"Love is universal, Dan. Without boundaries. It keeps things right in a world that has a lot of wrongs, especially at this time of year. That sled over there represents the unconditional love I received, first from my family, then from Bill, and I feel so fortunate just looking at it. Then there's Bobby. Such a happy, precious child could only have flourished in a home full of such love."

"Coming, Grampa?"

Dan looked at Bobby standing eagerly a few feet away. The lad was indeed precious. It wasn't a question of love, Dan told himself. He had always loved Lauren. Had never stopped loving her. Even after Sam . . . Dan felt the mental wall slam down that had allowed him to cope with losing Lauren, then Winnie.

As they walked home, Dan could hear Winnie saying, *You don't have a ghost of a chance.*

* * *

At Smiths Tree Farm Bobby flitted from tree to tree, claiming each one more beautiful than the last. Dan didn't mind. Walking in the pine-sharpened air in a snow-laden forest was, in his mind, the perfect way to spend a clear winter's day.

The Smiths operated a canteen, which, for the price of a donation to the Women's Shelter, provided hot chocolate, hotdogs, and cookies. Thus, what had been intended as a morning excursion wound up a full-day adventure. The moment they got home, Bobby pleaded to put the tree up right away.

"It'll be just fine on the porch until tomorrow," Dan said wearily. "And it'll be a lot easier to decorate after some pizza and a good night's sleep."

"Pizza? Okay!"

Note to self, Dan thought. When faced with an issue, use pizza. As they entered the house, the answering machine beeped a greeting. Bobby pulled off his boots and raced up to the phone.

Before Dan could tell him not to touch anything, Lauren's voice filled the house.

"Hi, Bobby, it's Mommy Lauren. We keep missing each other. But I really appreciate your calling me back. You sound so good, Bobby. Are you having fun with Grampa? I talked to Mom and she hopes to be home from Europe by the time we get back to Houston. Won't that be great? Well . . . take care. I'll try to reach you again tomorrow. Talk to you soon."

Dan sighed. Even if Lauren had spoken in a foreign tongue, he would have been able to tell by the happy lilt in her voice that her words had been directed at Bobby. Dan couldn't recall the last time she had used such a tone with him.

Hearing the message again brought Dan out of his despondency. He went up the stairs to find Bobby giggling into the machine.

"I think that's enough," Dan said as he stopped Bobby playing it a third time. The round face sagged with sadness and Dan looked for distraction. "We have to order pizza, right?"

"Oh yeah! Pizza!"

Relief mingled with his growing fatigue. Tonight, thought Dan, he would be retiring with Bobby.

* * *

After breakfast the next morning, Dan pulled boxes of decorations down from the attic where they had collected dust for the past three years. By lunch the tree was fully adorned. Winnie had always been the one to trim the tree, sometimes with help from Lauren. In later years, she had done it alone. The finished product always displayed a specific design. The arrangement in front of Dan revealed no such planning, but he had thoroughly enjoyed the numerous instructions and subsequent giggles from Bobby.

In spite of the chaotic result, Dan said, "I think your grandmother would have liked this tree."

Bobby, folding his arms into a posture similar to Dan's said, "I think so too. But what about all the decorations that are left?"

Dan thought of the cheer filling Annie's house. "Well,

I guess we could find a few places to put them. But let's have lunch first."

After their macaroni and cheese, which Dan had to admit tasted mighty fine, Bobby pulled open another box and dragged out a string of bulbs.

"They belong outside," Dan said.

"Where?"

"On the trees or perhaps over the garage . . ." Dan stopped at the gleam in Bobby's eyes. "Put your coat and boots on. And your snow pants too. It's chilly today."

By the time the sun set, both the interior of the house and the yard displayed their efforts. Some of the things that belonged outside Bobby had wanted inside, such as the big plywood snowman, which he stationed by the door to wish all visitors a merry Christmas. Some decorations that belonged indoors, such as tinsel, decorated the bushes lining the walkway.

But Dan didn't care. Everything, including the tree, exhibited a child's touch. And that was just fine. Be damned what the neighbors thought.

"What do you want for supper?" he asked.

"Pizza!"

"But we had pizza last night, and the night before."

Then Bobby said the magic words, "But the pizza in Houston isn't as good."

The pizza delivery lad had just left, smiling with his hefty tip, when the door bell rang again. Dan dropped the pizza on the kitchen table and returned to the front door.

Lauren stood in front of him. Shocked, he sputtered, "Lauren?"

She laughed nervously and gestured behind her. "I thought I went to the wrong house. Look at all this!"

"Mommy!" Bobby nearly knocked Dan over in his haste to reach Lauren.

Mommy, thought Dan. It sounded so right. A chilly

gust penetrated through his sweater. "Come in, both of you, before you catch cold!"

Bobby roughly yanked off Lauren's coat. He bounced around while she tried to hang it up. "How much sugar have you been having?" she asked.

"Only a little on my oatmeal!" Bobby squealed. "We've got pizza for supper again! And see the tree? Grampa and I cut it down an' then we had hot chocolate an' . . ."

Dan hastily steered them toward the kitchen. "Let's go eat the pizza while it's still hot. I hope this is all right," he added as he pulled Lauren's chair out.

"It looks delicious. I'm sorry I didn't call. I sold my last painting late yesterday and managed to get a flight out today. So I figured I'd just come." She glanced at Dan, as if asking if that was all right.

Dan wanted to reply that this was still her home, but his tongue felt too thick to talk.

"Good, huh?" Bobby mumbled, his cheeks puffed with pizza.

"Don't talk with your mouth full." Lauren picked up her knife and fork, her stiff actions displaying the tension Dan felt himself.

"Hmm," she said after swallowing. "This is just how I remember it. Tony's?"

"No, his son's."

"An' we had macaroni and cheese, and Grampa let me watch him push his snow machine, and I watched lots of television."

"Whoa! You don't have to tell your mother everything," Dan said. Like getting lost in the mall.

"But I want to!" Bobby squealed.

Oh Lord. Dan then realized how much he dreaded disappointing his daughter.

Lauren smiled as she patted Bobby's head. "He looks

great, Dad. Thanks."

"You're welcome."

Lauren held his gaze then, and Dan knew a moment had come. A moment in which he could really talk to his daughter, tell her how proud he was, how much he loved her. But when he felt his eyes water, he shifted his gaze to his plate. By the time he looked up, Lauren was wiping sauce off Bobby's shirt.

The moment had passed.

* * *

Dan got up the next morning filled with melancholy. He was about to lose his daughter once more. *But you never got her back*, he could hear Winnie saying.

When he heard movement from the floor above, he started cooking the oatmeal. By the giggle-accompanied bumps, he knew Lauren was packing up Bobby's things. Of course the boy was happy to be leaving. Soon he would be home with both his parents. Dan sighed and refused to think further along that line.

As Bobby devoured his oatmeal, Lauren toyed with hers and Dan ignored his. Good Lord, should it be this hard to converse with one's daughter? He said nothing as Bobby paused with his spoon over the brown sugar, looking for Dan's approval. Dan nodded and in spite of his mood, found himself laughing at Bobby's gleeful expression. Dan then caught Lauren eyeing him.

"What?" Dan asked, then without thinking said, "You can have more too."

Lauren's smile reached her eyes. "Ooh, thanks, Daddy!" She dipped the spoon into the sugar and stacked it high, causing Bobby to giggle loudly.

Dan's throat constricted and once more he felt dangerously close to tears. He sipped his coffee, hoping the dark liquid would be able to make it past his tight throat without sending him into a spasm of coughing.

Fortunately, Bobby's incessant babble filled the awkwardness. After piling the suitcases by the door, Dan helped Bobby into his snowsuit.

"Bye, tree!" Bobby yelled. "Bye, Lady!" he called up the stairs.

Lauren glanced upward, then at Dan, wrinkling her brow. Her nose almost joined the puzzlement, as it had in her younger years.

Dan tried to speak, but had to clear his voice first. "Bobby thought he saw a lady in your room."

"She told me to sleep with Grampa if I was scared."

Eager to change the subject, Dan looked at Bobby. "You said you were cold."

"I was cold, too."

Lauren pulled on Bobby's toque and smiled at him. "Maybe you had a dream about a lady."

That's right, Dan thought. A dream.

"Maybe," Bobby said as he thumped down the stairs. "I hope I dream of her again. She was nice." At the bottom of the stairs he pulled on his boots, adding, "After Grampa let me sleep with him, I didn't see her again."

To Dan's relief, Lauren said nothing further. Bobby's babble persisted all the way to the airport and spared Dan the effort at initiating conversation.

It took only moments to check them in but, when they rounded the corner to the security check, a line not dissimilar in length to one at a Disneyland ride greeted them.

"Ooh, this could take a while," Lauren said with a heavy sigh. "Good thing we're early."

Bobby, whose feet and body had danced and bounced all the way in from the parking lot, slumped to a stop, slapped his forehead and said, "Oh Lord!"

Startled, Dan looked at Lauren, then they both laughed. He drank in her lingering smile. She sobered and steered Bobby to the end of the line. Turning back, she said, "Look, Dad, you don't have to wait with us. Go on home."

Dan didn't want to go home. But he wasn't sure how long he could stay either. As the line inched slowly forward, Dan felt himself nearing an emotional cliff. Better go home before he lost it in front of Lauren and all these people.

Two small arms wrapped around his leg. "Bye, Grampa!"

His shrill squeal caused a lot of heads to turn Dan's way, but most of them were grinning. At that point Dan decided he wanted to hear a few more goodbyes. As many as possible, in fact. The distance between them grew then shortened again as they rounded a corner in the line.

When they were once more within a few feet, Dan desperately wanted to say "I love you," to the both of them, but just forming the words in his head brought him too close to the edge. No way could he voice them without breaking down. Dan instead focused on Bobby's cheerful face, trying to etch the features into permanent memory.

The lad tugged on his mother's arm. "Mommy Lauren? Can I ask Santa for something different?"

Dan edged closer, eager to hear what Bobby wanted. Maybe Lauren would let Grampa buy it. This thought cheered Dan considerably.

"Don't you want a Turboblaster?" Lauren asked.

Bobby's countenance sobered. "Yes. But I want

something more."

"What?"

"I want Grampa to see our Christmas tree. Can Santa bring him instead?"

Oh Lord. Dan's bottom lip began to quiver. He bit on it hard and turned toward the wall as tears flooded his eyes.

"Daddy?"

To his horror, Lauren sounded as if she was right behind him. She stepped under the rope and flung her arms around his neck. She sobbed into his ear. "That's what I want from Santa too!"

That did it. Dan squeezed his daughter tightly to him and cried uncontrollably into her hair. Tiny arms squeezed around Dan's legs and he put one hand onto the lad's head. Finally, he was able to choke out "I love you, Lauren," between sobs.

"Oh, Daddy, I love you too."

This brought another round of weeping between them. Gradually, as if in sync, the crying eased. Dan looked down at her. "Lauren . . ." His voice shook, but Dan persisted, determined to speak. "I'm so sorry!"

Lauren looked up at him, wiping her still streaming face with the back of her hand.

Dan took a deep breath and plunged ahead. "I've been so wrong. About you. About Sam." He looked down at Bobby and thought of Annie's words. "Look at this guy. What a great job you two have done. You're a wonderful mother, Lauren."

Lauren gushed more tears and pulled out tissues. "Thanks, Dad."

"Are those happy tears, Mommy?" Bobby asked with a worried frown.

"Definitely!" Lauren said with a brilliant smile at Dan. After she blew her nose, she said, "Well, what about it? I think Santa's sleigh will be too full to bring you. I could send you a ticket."

Dan looked at Bobby's expectant face. Why the hell not? Dan cleared his throat. "You-you'd better talk to Sam first."

Lauren laughed. "Are you kidding? From the very beginning she's been after me to get you to come to Houston. She's convinced she can win you over. I really want you to know her, Dad." Her eyes softened and widened. "Please?"

Dan swallowed. He had never been able to say no to that look.

"Please, Grampa?"

Dan glanced down to see Bobby sporting an exact replica of Lauren's expression. Dan laughed and nodded.

Lauren grabbed his arm. "Promise?"

Dan nodded again. "I'll go book my flight before I leave the airport."

Lauren and Bobby rejoined the line that had miraculously shortened. Not really a miracle, Dan surmised as he noticed two more security gates had opened. Way too soon, Bobby and Lauren passed through. He caught site of them on the other side.

"Grampa!" Bobby yelled. "Ask Santa for a Turboblaster!"

"I will!" Dan hollered back, to which Bobby leapt into the air, both hands reaching for the heavens. Oblivious to those around him, Bobby repeated this motion over and over as he and his still smiling mother disappeared around the corner.

Dan crossed the crowded lobby toward the ticket counter, feeling an incredible lightness. Only then did he realize the presence of everyone else had faded into unimportance. He could picture Winnie smiling that smile that had captured his heart the first time they met. Dan had no doubt that she had somehow played a role in this second chance with Lauren. Brilliant elation washed through him until he felt he was about to burst.

Instead, he leapt into the air, both hands reaching for the heavens.